HARLEQUIN

INTRIGUE®

FAMILIAR LULLABY

CAROLINE BURNES

D0034624

$4.25 U.S./$4.99 CAN.

A FEAR FAMILIAR MYSTERY

Get caught reading Harlequin.

Margaret Reynolds
813 Brooks Dr.
Midland, TX 79703

**THIS MONTH
GET CAUGHT READING
THESE HARLEQUIN
INTRIGUE® TITLES:**

#613 SOMEONE'S BABY
Dani Sinclair

#614 FAMILIAR LULLABY
Caroline Burnes

#615 CONCEPTION COVER-UP
Karen Lawton Barrett

#616 NO ONE BUT YOU
Carly Bishop

"Are you here alone?"

Lily bit her bottom lip. "Yes," she said. "I came out here for some privacy."

Something in the way she lowered her gaze made Mel suspicious. Lily wasn't a very good liar. Who was she protecting? His gaze drifted toward the stairs. He stood and walked that way.

Lily darted around him, blocking his path. "Unless you have a search warrant, you can't go there," she said.

She wasn't backing off an inch, and he felt his estimation of her rise. She was a pain to deal with, but he liked the way she handled herself. Mel took a step closer.

Lily held her ground and looked up at him. Her eyes were an amazing swirl of color. He found himself unable to glance away.

When he finally did, it was down to her lips. They were full and generous and just slightly parted. Almost as if they were awaiting a…kiss.

Way back in his brain, a tiny voice told him he was insane, that he was committing professional suicide, that he was acting on an impulse he would regret.

He didn't listen.

He lowered his lips slowly to hers.

Dear Harlequin Intrigue Reader,

All the evidence is in! And it would be a crime if you didn't "Get Caught Reading" this May. So follow the clues to your favorite bookstore to pick up some great tips.

This month Harlequin Intrigue has the distinguished privilege of launching a *brand-new* Harlequin continuity series with three of our top authors. TRUEBLOOD, TEXAS is a story of family and fortitude set in the great Lone Star state. We are pleased to give you your first look into this compelling drama with *Someone's Baby* by Dani Sinclair. Look for books from B.J. Daniels and Joanna Wayne to follow in the months ahead. You won't want to miss even a single detail!

Your favorite feline detective is back in *Familiar Lullaby* by Caroline Burnes. This time, Familiar's ladylove Clotilde gets in on the action when a baby is left on a high-society doorstep. Join a feisty reporter and a sexy detective as they search for the solution and find true love in this FEAR FAMILIAR mystery.

Our TOP SECRET BABIES promotion concludes this month with *Conception Cover-Up* by Karen Lawton Barrett. See how far a father will go to protect his unborn child and the woman he loves. Finally, Carly Bishop takes you out West for a showdown under a blaze of bullets in *No One But You*, the last installment in her LOVERS UNDER COVER trilogy.

So treat yourself to all four. You won't be disappointed.

Sincerely,

Denise O'Sullivan
Associate Senior Editor
Harlequin Intrigue

FAMILIAR LULLABY
CAROLINE BURNES

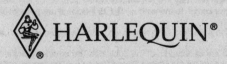

HARLEQUIN®

TORONTO • NEW YORK • LONDON
AMSTERDAM • PARIS • SYDNEY • HAMBURG
STOCKHOLM • ATHENS • TOKYO • MILAN • MADRID
PRAGUE • WARSAW • BUDAPEST • AUCKLAND

ISBN 0-373-22614-4

FAMILIAR LULLABY

Copyright © 2001 by Carolyn Haines

ABOUT THE AUTHOR

Caroline Burnes continues her life as doorman and can opener for her six cats and three dogs. E. A. Poe, the prototype cat for Familiar, rules as king of the ranch, followed by his lieutenants, Miss Vesta, Gumbo, Chester, Maggie the Cat and Ash. The dogs, though a more lowly life form, are tolerated as foot soldiers by the cats. They are Sweetie Pie, Maybelline and Corky.

Books by Caroline Burnes

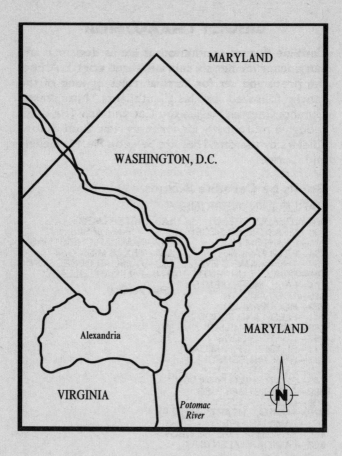

CAST OF CHARACTERS

Familiar—When a mysterious basket arrives on the feline detective's doorstep—and starts crying!—Familiar knows it's time to go to work.

Clotilde—Familiar's ladylove proves that a female kitty is always useful in times of crisis.

Lily Markey—The stubborn reporter will do what it takes to protect a mother and baby.

Mel Haskin—His past makes him doubly protective of an abandoned baby, and he knows Lily can help him solve the case—if she cooperates.

Susie Bishop—She made the ultimate sacrifice to save her baby.

Wayman Bishop—The mayor's slick right-hand man has his fingers in a lot of pies.

Jim Lavert—When a cop turns bad, there's nowhere to go but down.

Margie Lavert—Jim's widow is very helpful. Too helpful?

Rose and Preston Johnson—The wealthy couple has everything—except the child they've always longed for.

Baby David—The cause of all the ruckus.

To all of Familiar's fans, and especially to those who repeatedly asked to see more of Clotilde.

Chapter One

It's a party! Orchestra, glittering gowns, laughter, the sparkle of jewels and conversation. In attendance, the crème de la crème of Washington society. Not to be a name-dropper, but there's George Stephanopoulos. And over in the corner, another powerful pundit, George Will. Gads, none of the common reporter breed! And I see Senator Finances and the First Lady of Law and Order herself. Yes, Preston and Rose have created another successful power evening! Clotilde can be proud of her humanoids. I noticed earlier that the television vans were parked on the street. No working press invited tonight, but they'll be eager to film who comes in and out of the party.

Power, prestige and purr-fectly prepared food—this is absolutely the setting for a few smooth moves and some hanky-panky from a swanky black feline. Speaking of beauteous kitties, where is Clotilde? I'm out on the veranda, picnic spread, waiting to woo my love with sumptuous tidbits I've purloined from the various buffet tables. And Clotilde keeps me waiting. Isn't that just like a feline?

So I have a little time to recheck the menu. I have some smoked salmon with cream cheese spread and caviar. A little salty for my taste, but Clotilde loves it. Honestly, the way that caterer acted when he caught me snatching it off the table, you'd think it was gold bullion.

Now some escargots—yum. Fascinating what garlic and butter will do for a snail. A bit of beef, a sampling of roasted pork, some cheeses. I'd say I covered all the bases. As for dessert, that's something I want to save for later, if you get my drift.

The night is a little chill for the humanoids, which means they'll stay inside. Clotilde and I will have the lovely veranda all to ourselves. We can still hear the music and watch the bipeds do the dance of power and politics. And we can dine at leisure, without censure or interruption. Goodness, after my last case in New Orleans I'm glad to be home. I think I might have to take a breather from the P.I. business. I think a few weeks of Clotilde...what's that?

Someone is climbing over the wall in Preston's backyard. The guest list was exclusive, but I hardly think this party is worth breaking and entering. A sleek, elegant black shadow—hey, it could be me if I were a biped. Except this one is a woman! I wonder if it's one of those pushy media types.

No, she's carrying a basket. A big basket. And she's being very, very careful not to be seen. I think this must be one of those surprise delivery services. You know, the ones that drop off expensive gifts in deadly secret. Let me say, I highly approve of this delivery gal. She's got a pair of gams that Ginger Rogers would envy—long, lean and well-muscled. And the torso sitting on top of them screams "kick-boxing fool." She climbed that wall like it wasn't twelve feet of solid cement. And she can crouch and run—a talent for a biped, and don't forget it.

The basket is pretty heavy, too. And she's leaving it on the veranda. Very stealthy lady. A secret gift basket. Someone has sent Clotilde's humans a lovely basket of food for the party. And guess what! I'm going to make sure there's nothing in there that might make a humanoid sick. That's part of my feline duties—to consume any suspicious foodstuffs. I'll just give batwoman another second to fly back over the wall.... Now I can make my move on the food basket. I hope it's a good, salty ham. It looked to weigh about ten pounds or so.

There's just nothing like a ham—uh, oh, this ain't no smoked piglet. It's alive and kicking, and it's about to start crying for mama. That woman abandoned a baby! A real, live humanoid of the smaller version. A humanette. A muchacha. A bambino. A babette.

Oh, my goodness. It's so newborn its eyes can't focus. She can't see Uncle Familiar hovering over her. And it's too cool out on this veranda for a baby! What was that woman thinking?

Thank goodness, here's Clotilde. One look at the little bambino and I can see a plan in her eyes. Yes, I know Rose and Preston have wanted a baby for years. Yes, I know they'd make perfect, loving parents. Yes, I know they could give a child all the advantages.

But that doesn't negate the fact that this child belongs to someone—someone who climbed a wall and dumped it here.

Clotilde has found a note. And the baby is starting to cry. Much as I hate to do it, I think I'm going to have to find Eleanor. Clotilde wants to keep this baby, but whoever abandoned a child deserves to be punished. Severely punished.

A lot of people view living creatures as disposable. If they don't want a kitten, or a puppy or a baby, they just throw it away—toss it out somewhere and hope someone will find it and want it.

Or toss it out and just let it die of starvation.

This burns me up! I know, from personal experience, what it feels like to be tossed. And though Clotilde may view this as a gift from God, the long-legged humanoid who brought this baby here is soon going to view me as the avenging angel. Okay, here's Eleanor. She'll know what to do to keep the little whippersnapper from crying so.

MEL HASKIN leaned against the wall and took in his surroundings. Enough food for an army lay deserted on buffet tables where chilled bottles of champagne still resided in ice buckets. Yes, this was one party that had come to a screeching halt. And all for the little bundle that a handsome, dark-haired couple hovered over.

Eleanor Curry taped the diaper into place and then relinquished the baby to Rose Johnson.

"I'm a veterinarian, not a pediatrician," Peter Curry

said, "but that baby isn't more than ten hours old. He's been well taken care of."

"There's a note, officer." Eleanor glanced at the woman with the infant as she picked up the note and read aloud. "'His name is David. He has the power to slay Goliath, and you must protect him from his enemies. Keep him safe and always remind him of his mother's love and her sacrifice to protect him.'"

"I will protect him. We will." Rose Johnson cradled the baby in her arms and looked up to meet her husband's gaze. He nodded firmly.

"Rose, a crime has been committed," Eleanor reminded her. "You can't keep this baby."

"Watch me," Rose said. She settled on the sofa with the child in her arms and the beautiful calico cat purring at her side. "Even Clotilde thinks he belongs to us."

Mel gingerly took the note that Eleanor Curry offered him.

"I'm afraid it's been handled by quite a few people," Eleanor said apologetically. "When Familiar found the baby, we all became a little excited. We passed the note around the party. It's just that...well, we weren't actually thinking of the baby as a crime at the time."

"No one saw the drop?" Mel asked. He personally was avoiding the baby. It wasn't that he didn't like children. In fact, one day he hoped to have a couple. But with the work he did, he viewed babies and small children as victims. They had no voice, no way to protect themselves against whatever rotten deal their worthless parents happened to hand out to them.

Just like the baby in this case. So what if the mother had named him—the Biblical name of a young man who slew a giant? And so what if she'd left him on the doorstep of a wealthy home—a place where he was obviously wanted and would have every advantage?

None of that made a difference. Not to him. No matter how the facts were dressed up, the story was the same. Some young woman had gotten herself pregnant and had the kid. Then because the kid would inconvenience her life, she'd dumped the responsibility on someone else.

In Mel's book, that was a crime that deserved prosecution. And he was just the man to do it.

"Meow."

He was pulled from his thoughts by sharp claws in his shin. He looked down into the green eyes of the sleekest black cat he'd ever seen.

"Meow."

"What?" He looked around to make sure no one had heard him talking to the cat.

The cat turned quickly and went to the basket, which had been put beside the sofa. With one expressive black paw, the cat patted the basket.

Mel picked it up and examined it. His fingers brushed against the blanket the baby had been wrapped him. Soft. Very soft. He pulled the pale blue wrap out of the basket and shook it out. He'd never felt a baby blanket so soft. His fingers rubbed the texture. Cashmere! Incredible.

And the cat was tipping the basket over to indicate a tag. He looked at it. Not just an ordinary wicker basket—this one was signed. A handmade basket. Now that was a clue. As discreetly as possible he returned the blanket to the basket.

"I'd like to take these items as evidence," he said.

"I'd prefer that you didn't," Rose Johnson said quickly. "Those may be all this little boy has to remember his mother by. I'd like to hold on to them and give them to him when he's older."

Mel sighed. He was going to have his hands full now. In her mind, Mrs. Johnson had adopted this child. She was already planning his future.

"The baby will have to be taken to DHR," he said as gently as he could. "It's the law, ma'am."

"Surely we can work something out, detective," Preston Johnson said, stepping forward. "We'll assume complete responsibility for this child." He put his hands on his wife's shoulders. "We'll hire a full-time nurse, if that would help. We'll start a college fund."

Mel held up a hand. "I don't doubt that you'd make the most wonderful parents in the world. But that's not up to me to decide. I'm only a detective. The Department of Human Resources handles all of these cases. All I do is follow the procedure."

He saw the frown pass over Preston Johnson's face and knew these weren't people who gave up easily. Too bad the baby's mother hadn't wanted him one-tenth as much as these strangers. He felt a flush of fury. At a strange woman. At the cruelty of fate.

"Detective, I don't mean to usurp your authority," Preston said carefully. "Would it offend you if I made a call to Judge Patterson? I believe he handles these cases, and we're old friends. If he said we could keep the child—just until Monday morning—would you feel comfortable with that?"

Normally, Mel knew the suggestion of going over his head to a judge would ignite his sense of outrage. But for some reason—probably because the Johnsons so obviously cared for this abandoned baby—he felt only hope. "Judge Patterson has the final say. If he gives me the green light to leave the baby, I'll do it with a glad heart."

Preston Johnson smiled. "I'll make the call. While you're waiting, could we make you some coffee? I'd offer champagne, since we had to hustle all of our guests out the door." He chuckled. "But I know you're on duty."

"Coffee would be nice," Mel said. Actually, he just wanted to get back to the department, where he'd left a stack of paperwork a mile high on the last case he'd finished. A double homicide. What he wanted more than anything was ten consecutive hours of sleep.

Everyone else in the room was so involved with the baby they failed to hear the disturbance at the front door. Curious, Mel slipped out of the room, down the hallway and to the front where the butler held firmly to the door.

"I'm sorry, miss, but no press was allowed to attend tonight. I don't believe the Johnsons want to change that policy now."

"I heard that someone dropped a baby."

Mel recognized the crisp tones of the reporter and he stifled a groan. Lily Markey. She was a pitbull disguised as a fashion model. Of all the hundreds of reporters in Washington, D.C., Lily Markey was the one he dreaded most. She wasn't unethical, and she wasn't sensational—what she was was a pain in the butt because she was *so* ethical. She had a reputation for being tough but fair, and she lived up to it every day. In a city where law enforcement viewed most of the media as egotists and liars, Lily had everyone's respect.

And here she was with a tip about the baby.

"Miss, you can call Mr. Johnson Monday at his office. I'm sure he'll talk with you."

"It's Saturday night. I can't wait until Monday," Lily said sweetly. "In fact, I've got an hour until deadline. I have to see one of the Johnsons right this minute."

"Impossible," the butler said sternly. "Now remove yourself or I'll have to take appropriate steps."

Mel sighed again. He could deal with Lily now, or he could wait until later, but deal with her he'd have to. He walked up to the door. "I'll take care of this," he said softly to the butler. "Thanks."

He opened the door, stepped outside and closed the door behind him.

"Mel?" Lily showed genuine surprise. "The baby's okay, isn't he?"

Mel was struck first by Lily's intensity. She was a woman who gave her heart and soul to her work. He noticed her beauty and her word choice almost as a simultaneous second.

"He? You must have one helluva source at the department because I haven't phoned in the gender of the baby to anyone."

He'd caught her off guard, and he was pleased to see her flush. Lily Markey had a very powerful source. Someone way high on the food chain in law enforcement was feeding her facts. And he'd nailed her on it.

"Oops," she said, biting her bottom lip in a way that said she was a silly child. Only Mel knew she wasn't silly, and she wasn't a child.

"Oops is right. With a clue like that, I might be able to figure out who your source is."

"Unlikely," she said, recovering her balance. "Now tell me about the baby. Will the Johnsons keep hi—it?"

"How did you know—"

"I've been to numerous cocktail parties thrown by Rose and Preston. Everyone in their circle knows how much they want a child." Lily waved one graceful hand in the air, dismissing the personal knowledge she'd obtained.

"Even a *Washington Post* political reporter?" Mel didn't bother to hide the sarcasm in his voice. Sane people, especially those who lived in the fishbowl of Washington politics, would gnaw off an arm before allowing a media person to know any of their personal business. Especially something as private as a desire for a child.

"I'm not an ogre. I can understand the desire for a child."

There was a defensive tone in Lily's voice and Mel wondered if he'd hit a nerve. "I thought it was newspaper policy that you had to eat at least three of your young to prove you were tough enough."

To his surprise she laughed. "Old policy. The newspaper revamped with a kinder, gentler policy. Now we just have to eat three police detectives."

"Touché," he said, laughing also. He couldn't help but notice that Lily, though reputed to be cold and heartless, had eyes that danced with merriment when she laughed. With her auburn hair and green eyes, she seemed more Irish lass at the moment than big-city reporter.

He changed his mind instantly when she opened her mouth. "So, what about the baby? Will the Johnsons keep it?"

"That's to be determined by DHR," he said, stepping back into his official role.

"What are you doing here? I thought criminal action was your bailiwick?"

"It is. There's nothing more criminal than abandoning a child."

"Abandoning?"

He narrowed his gaze at Lily. She acted as if he'd said the baby had been abused.

"I thought it was left here at the Johnson home. During a big party. That doesn't seem to constitute abandonment. I mean, it isn't as if someone left him out in the freezing cold in a Dumpster or—"

"That baby was abandoned as surely as if the mother dropped him in an alley like an unwanted kitten."

"I beg to differ. I—"

To Mel's surprise, Lily halted in mid-sentence. She bit her bottom lip again, as if to force herself to shut up.

"Why does it seem to me that you've got a personal stake in this baby?" He was only playing a hunch, but his hunches were one of the reasons he was considered one of the top three detectives in Washington, D.C.

"It's just a terrific human-interest story."

"I thought politics was your beat." He felt that strange tingling that made every one of his senses come alive.

"It is. The Johnsons are political."

"An unwanted baby isn't exactly what I'd consider your normal turf." He paused. "What are you doing here, Lily?"

She hesitated. "I'll tell you, Mel. I got this tip from a friend. A close friend. I was asked to pursue the story, as a personal favor."

He nodded. That made a little more sense. "Well, there's no story here yet."

"Level with me. The baby's okay, right?"

There was worry in her voice though she did her best to hide it. "Yes. He seems fine. The Johnsons have called a doctor to check him out. It would appear the infant will have every benefit that money can buy. At least for the short amount of time the Johnsons can keep him."

"What do you mean? They want him, don't they?"

"You may know the Johnsons, but you aren't familiar with the law. A person can't just find a baby and keep it because she wants it. The baby will have to go through the system."

"But the Johnsons would make terrific parents."

"That'll be for DHR and a judge to determine. I'm afraid the baby is going to spend the first few months of his life in an institution." He heard the bitterness in his tone even though he'd thought he was long over it. He saw that Lily, too, heard it. She gave him a speculative look but said nothing else.

"Could I speak to the Johnsons?" she asked.

"Give me your card. I'll leave it with them. Right now, I can honestly tell you that they're interested only in the baby."

Lily smiled. "That's good to know."

"Yeah," Mel said. "It is."

He took the business card she offered and watched as she strode down the walk with long, bold steps. She was tall, slender and athletic. Just the kind of woman that could rock his world.

He turned back to the house and found that he wasn't alone on the steps. The black cat was sitting beside his feet, tail twitching. The cat watched the departing newspaper reporter with green-eyed intensity.

It seemed he wasn't the only one with hunches on a cold March night.

Chapter Two

Lily Markey forced her shoulders up and back and walked away from the Johnson house with her head high and her stride purposeful. It took all of her inner strength to do so.

Of all the luck! Mel Haskin! What trick of fate had put a homicide detective on a baby case? And damn it all, he acted as if he was taking the abandonment personally!

She got in her car and slammed the door, locking it against a March wind that had grown a lot colder since three hours ago, when she'd made her first visit of the evening to the Johnson home.

She closed her eyes and leaned back against the headrest, trying to ease the tension in her neck. She'd dropped off the baby just as she'd promised. And David had been found. He was safe. Inside that big house with people who wanted him. People who would give him a future and every advantage. He would never be in danger of being hit or used as a pawn in an ugly domestic power game.

Her hands gripped the steering wheel, and she

waited for the anxiety to pass. When she felt steadier, she started the car and drove away.

She'd done the best thing. She'd done the only thing. She'd done what was right for David, and for his mother. But it wasn't over yet. Not by a long shot.

David was safe. Now she had to make certain that the frightened young woman who'd entrusted her newborn to Lily had a shot at a decent life, too.

MEL SAW THE LOOK of happiness on Preston Johnson's face and knew that the judge had ruled in favor of leaving the baby in the Johnson home.

"He made it clear it wasn't permanent," Preston said. "But each hour we keep this baby strengthens our case, don't you think?"

Mel kept his opinion to himself. The legal system didn't always seem to work in a rational or kind-hearted, way. Based on what he'd seen of the Johnsons, he'd vote to leave baby David here until college age. But he wasn't in charge. He was just a cog in the big system.

"Judge Patterson told us we had to appear Monday morning," Preston said. "We'll be there."

"Yes." Rose Johnson stood. "Thank you, detective. And if you do find the mother, maybe you could…"

He knew what she wanted. Maybe he could put in a word and say what a good home the baby would have. "I'll do what I can," he said. "I'll be in touch."

He checked the room once more. The Johnsons and their friends, the Currys, were involved with the baby.

Even the strange cats, the black and the calico, were acting as if a little prince had dropped from the sky. Maybe there were still homes where people loved children and pets.

He hurried back out into the night. He had work to do at his office. And he also wanted to make a few calls. In his years on the streets he'd developed a few contacts, but what good would they do him in this case? Someone had delivered this baby, but he was willing to bet it wasn't a teenager who'd gone through the labor process alone. The baby had been cleaned, the navel properly attended. And there was the expensive blanket and basket. No, this baby came from money.

And now his interest was piqued.

LILY SAT in the chair beside the bed. She put a hand on Susie Bishop's forehead and was relieved to discover she was cool to the touch. No fever. That was good. Of course, nothing could ease the pain in Susie's expression as she opened her eyes.

"They wanted my baby?" Her voice broke on the words and Lily found her own eyes misting with tears. Some tough reporter she was. If any of the guys in the newsroom saw her, she'd be laughed out of the building.

"They fell in love with him. Of course, they'll have to get legal custody." She let it drop there. She'd miscalculated twice already—once in delivering the baby during a party and next in assuming that the Johnsons wouldn't report the baby. She'd simply assumed they'd enfold the child into the bosom of their family. In that she'd been wrong.

"Is something the matter?" Susie asked.

Lily instantly smiled. "Of course not. Everything's just like I said it would be. Now you have to concentrate on getting up and moving. We have to get you out of the city, Susie."

The woman turned her face away. "And go where? He'll find me. He said it didn't matter where I went, he'd always find me. And he'd make me pay."

Lily felt the bracing power of anger. "He can *say* anything he wants, but he isn't omnipotent. He doesn't control Washington. I'll get you out of this town. There's a big world out there, Susie. And there're lots of nice people, too. Like you."

"He has his finger in every pie in town. Half the police force seems to be on his private payroll."

Lily felt dread course through her body. Mel Haskin. The word on the street was that Mel couldn't be bought. But the old saying was that every man had his price. If Mel ever got a hint of who baby David really was, disaster would surely follow.

"Look, Susie. Don't worry about that now. Rest. I've got to go to the newspaper and finish a story. I'll come back with some food and then you're going to get up and walk. Remember. That's what the midwife said. Walk, walk, walk. But wait for me, okay?"

"Why are you doing this? If Wayman finds out you helped me, he can make your life a living hell." Her voice broke. "If there's any life left in you. He'll kill you, Lily."

"He won't find out." Lily wiped the tear away from Susie's cheek. She was so weak, so beaten down. The trace of a bruise still lay under the skin of her cheek. What had it been, a week ago that Wayman Bishop had thrown his nine-months-pregnant wife into a wall because his coffee got cold before he drank it?

"He's so mean." Her voice was barely a whisper.

"I can be mean, too. If I have to." She smiled and patted Susie's head. "I know judo, karate, and I won the kick-boxing championship. Lemme at 'im."

Her bravado was rewarded with a weak smile from Susie. "I wish I was half as brave as you are."

"You are, Susie. You saved your baby. That took incredible courage. You gave that little boy a chance for a life of love, even though it meant you had to lose him."

"Wayman would have ruined him. He would have beaten him, or he would have turned him into a mean bully. Either way, I couldn't stand it."

"Hush now. Just rest. I'll be back in no more than two hours."

THE HOUSE is settling down for a much-deserved nap. Even Clotilde is yawning, but I can see that she has something on her mind. There's one thing about cats— once they focus in on something, there's no stopping them. I've seen foolish humanoids attempt to train a cat to stay off a counter. Newspaper, water pistols— hah! Tools of an incompetent! There is nothing that can dissuade a cat. The only thing to do is to remove whatever object has drawn the cat's interest. Voila— problem solved.

Unless, of course, the cat just happens to enjoy toying a bit with the bipeds in the house. That's been known to happen more than once. And then there are those cats who worry about their humanoids. Like Clotilde. I can tell by her twitching tail that she's in a twist.

"What is it, Clotilde, my love?

"You're worried about your humans? You think they'll fall in love with baby David and then he'll be taken away from them?

"You want me to do what?"

Geez, I've just come off a case, and now she wants me to track down the humanoid who gave birth to baby David. That isn't going to be an easy thing to do. Women who dump babies generally don't want to be found. And already Detective Dick Tracy is on the case. Boy, did he have an attitude or what? I could see it from a mile off. Every time he looked at that baby he got righteous.

Yet he seemed to have a real tender spot. Maybe he just didn't want to work an abandoned baby case. Probably a step down for a homicide detective. Me, on the other hand, I like it when all the players in the game are still alive.

But who says the mother is alive? Holy moly, what if she was murdered and the baby taken and then dumped? I can see that Clotilde is reading my expression and not liking a single thing she sees. Humanoids think that I'm inscrutable, but Clotilde can read me like a book. So I'd better change the content of my thoughts.

"Nothing, love. I was just thinking about how to find David's mama. The blanket and basket are good clues. Dick Tracy noticed them also. And he took them with him when he left. If I wait around, he'll do the legwork for me...."

"What, precious? You want me to start tonight— before the police find her? And you're going to help me?!"

Aye caramba—why do I suddenly feel like Ricky Ricardo when Lucy decided to help him with his career? But the best thing to do is smile and play along.

"That would be great. We could work together. Familiar and Clotilde. Yes, that does have a nice ring to it."

Brother, I'm in way deep now. I guess we're going out to search the backyard for additional clues.

MEL CLOSED the files on his desk with a sigh. Within the time frame he'd established, he couldn't find a single record of a baby of David's size and gender born in any of Washington's hospitals that wasn't accounted for.

So that meant a midwife or some other type of health-services delivery. Private clinic. He'd heard of places where wealthy women went to have their children; places with all the frills of a health spa plus the benefit of top physicians. Lots of celebrities opted for these exclusive, and very private, facilities.

Or there was the possibility of the extreme opposite—cheap hotel room and midwife. Somehow, though, that just didn't fit with baby David.

This case was going to take a lot of legwork. And, suddenly, he didn't want to pursue it. Hell, the baby had a good home. He was safe and wanted. If the system acted in a logical way, David would soon legally be David Johnson, only child of loving parents.

Maybe he should drop it.

Sitting in the busy police station, Mel looked down at his scarred desk. When he'd been three or four, he'd eaten at a table that was nicked and scarred. Him and six dozen other boys. They'd eaten three meals a day there, even when money was short and the food served was oatmeal—morning, noon and night.

It wasn't the food that Mel remembered with a clenched stomach. It was the long nights of being afraid, of wondering if his mother would come for him. She'd promised him that she'd come back for him. Soon. But weeks had passed. Then months. Then years. And she never came back.

He'd never seen her again. She was just a memory—a tall, slender woman walking down the hallway, her legs moving as fast as they possibly could as she hurried away from him. As she got near the end of the hallway, she'd begun to run—right into her new life. Leaving him behind. An orphan. A child that no one wanted.

No, he couldn't drop it. Not on his life.

"Hey, Mel. What's going on?" Sonny Caruso dropped his coat on the chair by the desk next to Mel.

"Not much."

"You looked like you were planning a bombing, or at least a hijacking. Very big thundercloud on your forehead, buddy."

Mel forced a smile. Sonny Caruso was a handsome, dark-haired detective who had more natural intuition that most women. And the one thing Mel didn't want was Sonny poking into his past.

"Got an abandoned baby. What are you working on?" Mel leaned back in his chair, forcing his body language to be casual.

"You'll love this. We had a woman killed downtown. Beaten to death. Probably a working girl, but she was dressed a little odd. Sort of business suit, so we couldn't be certain. I put in a call on the radio, notified forensics, etcetera, and guess who shows up?"

"Who?"

"The number-one advisor to the mayor, Wayman Bishop. He was all over the scene like white on rice."

"Doing what?" Mel was intrigued. Wayman Bishop, who advised Mayor Al Torrell on all things of importance in the city of Washington, D.C., was less concerned about crime in the city than he was about litter. The death of a victim normally wouldn't ruffle a hair on his head—unless it might have political repercussions.

"Nosing around, hunting for facts about 'the heinous crime.'"

"I hate to be cynical, but it sounds like Mayor Torrell is getting ready to gear up some kind of antiviolence campaign. He's building his base for the next election. It's easy to be against crime. What's hard is doing something to prevent it.''

"Exactly what I thought," Sonny said. He looked into the coffee cup sitting on his desk, made a face and threw the whole thing into the trash. "My wife told me to buy disposable cups. She said I'd never wash mine out. She was right.''

"How is Louann?" Mel liked Sonny's wife. She was a cartoonist, still waiting for a break with a syndicated strip or some steady income.

"She's fine. Working all the time. She'll get a break eventually.''

Mel nodded, but his mind was back on the dead woman and the mayor's advisor. "So what did Bishop do, have the mayor's picture taken with the dead woman?''

Sonny laughed. "You have a macabre sense of humor, buddy. No, he just lurked around, taking notes. He finally got a look at the woman and then he split like he'd been shot at.''

"Any suspects on the murder?''

"Usual ones. Spouse, boyfriend, neighbor, pimp, unhappy customer. You know, fill in the blank." Sonny shook his head. "This job makes it difficult to love my fellow man.''

"I know what you mean," Mel said. "Somebody dropped off a baby at a social event.''

"No kidding." Sonny's dark eyebrows lifted almost to his hairline. "Posh party?''

"Preston Johnson's.''

"Very posh," Sonny said. "Plenty of money to

give a kid a good home. But they won't keep an abandoned baby.''

"They will, if they can. That's the good news," Mel said. "I'm just wondering how the natural mother might have known that the Johnsons wanted a child. See, the more I look into this, the more I get that gut feeling that the Johnsons were carefully selected. Whoever put little David in the basket and left him on that doorstep knew exactly what she was doing.''

"The plot thickens, eh?" Sonny said.

"Yeah," Mel agreed. "The plot thickens, and I want it up to a real good boil when I find the woman who dumped her kid.''

He saw the curious look return to Sonny's eyes and realized his tone had been a lot harsher than he intended. He stood up, picked up his coat and headed toward the door. "I'm going to run some leads. Good luck with your homicide.''

"You bet." Sonny waved goodbye as he reached for the computer mouse and began his own work.

Mel was at a loss for the moment. It would take days to find all the private clinics around Washington, and then collect warrants to search their records. He doubted his superiors would put that much time, manpower and effort into finding a woman who'd thrown her baby away. No, Mel was going to have to work this case mostly on his own.

And to do so effectively, he would have to play his hunches.

He got in his car and drove over to the brightly lit building that housed one of the nation's most powerful newspapers. When he found a comfortable spot to watch the employee parking lot, he settled down and waited for Lily Markey to appear.

LILY GATHERED UP her things from her desk at the *Post* and was almost away from her desk when she heard her boss clear his throat behind her.

"When can I expect that story on white-collar spousal abuse?" he asked.

"I'm working on it." Lily tucked her notebook in her purse.

"What's the holdup?" Bill Smith asked.

"I'm…waiting for an interview to gel." Lily finally met his gaze. More than anything she wanted to tell her boss the truth, but it was too dangerous. She'd crossed the line from journalist to activist, and Susie Bishop's safety hung in the balance. If she ran the story on spousal abuse now, it would be a red flag to Wayman Bishop.

"Is there something you need to tell me?" Bill asked. He was a tall man with salt-and-pepper hair and above-average intelligence.

"Not right now." She dropped her gaze. "I'll get the story. You know I always do."

"You're reputation isn't in question, Lily. I'm just wondering why you're acting like a cat on a hot tin roof." His look was astute and calculating.

"Gotta go, Bill." She flashed him a smile, albeit a forced one. "I have an interview and it may be the icing on the cake." She thought of something truthful she could add. "I told you when I thought of doing this story that it might be Pulitzer material. I still think that. But I need time to be sure that I get everything just right.''

''You've got the time, Lily. Just don't step off in water over your head. You're up to something. I'm just not sure what it is.''

She didn't bother to answer. Prevarication wasn't her favorite form of communication, especially with a man she respected as much as Bill Smith. She headed out the door of the newsroom and straight to the grocery store where she picked up some items she hoped would make Susie Bishop a little more comfortable. She didn't notice the gray sedan that fell in behind her as she drove toward one of Washington's worst districts.

Chapter Three

Lily slowed her car to a near crawl as she turned right on Cedar Street. The name was so inappropriate that she allowed herself a bitter chuckle. If there had ever been a tree—or even a blade of grass—along this street, none of the residents had lived long enough to remember it.

Whatever green and lovely visions had inspired the name of Cedar Street were long gone. All that remained was bleak pavement, torn and twisted chain-link fencing, broken bottles and broken streetlights. It looked as if a war had been fought in the not-too-distant past and the street abandoned. The only sign of life was the blue flicker of a few television screens in the windows of the run-down homes that she passed.

A flash of car lights in the rearview mirror got her attention. She instantly tensed, her hand checking the automatic door lock to be sure she'd clicked it on. In the otherwise deserted street, the approaching car seemed dangerous.

She pulled to the curb and waited, noting that the car had hesitated, then picked up speed as it drew abreast of her. She looked at the solitary driver, feeling a sense of shock at the profile she recognized. Detective Mel Haskin. And he was pulling up ahead of her.

Fear of being injured instantly gave way to anger. Why was the policeman following her? She was a law-abiding citizen—at least, most of the time. Why was Mel so obviously tailing her? And why hadn't she paid more attention to who was behind her?

At his approach she rolled down her window. "You'd better have a damn good reason for following me, or at the very least a search warrant for my car."

Mel didn't answer immediately. His gaze swept over the interior of the car, and Lily was glad she'd put the groceries in the trunk. Though the items were innocuous enough, there were things that might make him believe she was visiting someone who was sick.

"This is a dangerous neighborhood, Lily. I hope you have a good reason for being here."

She was surprised at his use of her given name. "Good enough, and also personal. What are you doing here? Is it Detective Haskin or Mel?" She saw that he registered her point. And by his next words, she knew he had ignored it.

"I'm following you."

His bluntness made her take a deep breath. Had he found out about David? What was he going to do? "What? Do I have an outstanding parking ticket?" She decided to bluff her way through the situation.

"Try again."

"I know. I didn't pay for my tickets to the policeman's ball." She put another degree of unpleasantness in her voice.

"Give it one more try." Mel Haskin, on the other hand, was using the condescending tone of a man talking to a child.

"You tell me," Lily said, very angry.

"Suspicious behavior," he said casually.

"You'll have to do better than that," Lily said. "I've got a right to be anywhere I choose, as long as I'm not violating the law. I also have a right not to be harassed by the police."

"Reporters all seem to think they have a lot more rights than other people," Mel said, his tone still conversational, though his dark eyes crackled with intensity.

"I'll give you one more chance. What do you want? Either tell me or leave me alone. If you don't comply, I'll have to go to your superior and explain that you've been following me and harassing me."

"You do that—and while you're there, I want you to explain to my superior what you're doing in this part of town late at night. This is a far cry from the posh neighborhood where the Johnsons reside. I'm just wondering if your presence in both places somehow links them together."

"I'm working on a story. I'm doing my job." Lily's heart rate had tripled, but she knew she had to keep Mel from seeing the effect he was having on her.

"I'd believe that if it had been the body of a dead politician that was discovered on the Johnsons' veranda. Or, say, a woman who was having an affair with one of the Washington officials. Or even the son or daughter of some official who wanted to spill the beans on good old mom or dad.'' He paused for effect. ''Those things I'd believe—they're what the media today consider legitimate stories.''

''I work on several stories at the same time. Reporters don't have the luxury of focusing on a single story.''

Mel laughed a deep, full laugh that under other circumstances might have triggered a smile on Lily's face. Instead, her frown deepened.

''I'm just curious about what the *Post*'s premier political reporter has to say about a baby. Yes, a baby is a legitimate story. Readers love stories with fairy-tale endings, and if the Johnsons adopt that baby, he'll have a wonderful life. I just don't see you as the reporter to put that Cinderella finish on it, though. You're too tough.''

''You're getting very close to being insulting.'' Lily was shocked that he could get under her skin. Being tough was usually a compliment, but Mel made her sound cold and hard and heartless.

''I didn't realize you were such a romantic, Lily. Reading your byline in the paper, I always had the feeling you were more interested in being the executioner than the fairy godmother.''

His words stung, and Lily tightened her hands on the steering wheel. Though one part of her brain knew he was trying to goad her into a response, she couldn't stop herself. ''That's a damn lie. I don't identify with the executioner. When people do bad things, I write about it. Just exactly the same way you try to put them in jail.'' The more she talked, the hotter she got. She pushed her door open, forcing him to step back, as she got out of the car.

''I didn't realize you were so sensitive,'' Mel said, his amusement only further inflaming her.

''I'm not overly sensitive. I'm a hardworking reporter who tries to write the best story she can find. I don't make up facts and I don't persecute individuals, but by God if I get the goods on them, then I don't cry in my coffee when I hang them out to dry in print.''

''What terrible deed can you pin on an infant?'' he asked.

''Not the infant, you nitwit. The fa—'' She barely caught herself in time. ''What's this personal vendetta you have against me?''

''It's not personal, Lily. I just want to know what your role is regarding the abandoned baby. Right about now, I'm sure you have one.''

She inhaled sharply and knew she had to gather her wits and keep her mouth shut. Mel Haskin was a superb interrogator, and he'd just gotten her to admit some very important information about her private views on life.

''My role is to write a story about this baby, if there's a story worth writing. And I won't know that until I look into the facts a little more. So tell me, Detective, why are you following me? And this time I won't be distracted. I want the truth.''

''I think you know more about this baby than you're

letting on. See, I don't buy it that the *primo* political reporter for the paper is suddenly going to write a women's-section story about abandoned kids. I know the newspaper business. You've worked hard to be respected as a political journalist. You don't want to go back to writing touchy-feely pieces on babies.''

Although Mel angered her, Lily had to give him credit for understanding her business far better than she'd ever have thought. She'd busted her chops getting accepted as a political writer. Even though journalism was an area where women rose farther and faster than most other professions, there was still a glass ceiling.

Even if she'd wanted to write a ''touchy-feely piece,'' as Mel put it, she couldn't afford to show that kind of weakness.

''That still doesn't tell me why you're tailing me.'' She had to get the focus of the conversation off her and back where it belonged—on Mel.

''Like I said, I'm curious to see what you're up to. I'm playing a hunch.''

''That borders on harassment.'' She could see she wasn't calling his bluff.

''I don't think my boss or your lawyer would agree.''

''I don't like being followed.''

Mel nodded. ''I'll note your objections. If you want me to stop, why don't you tell me what you know about this mysterious baby?''

Lily felt her frustration grow. She'd already wasted fifteen minutes with the detective. Susie was waiting for her. Waiting and probably fretting. And she had to figure out how to write her story without putting Susie in more danger.

"I have a busy night planned, officer. Now, if you'll excuse me...."

She felt his hand on her arm. "What are you doing down here?" He nodded at the street, which was no longer empty. Several shadowy figures had appeared at the end of the block, and they were standing and waiting, like wolves packed for the kill.

Looking at the four men, Lily felt a tremor of fear shoot through her. The neighborhood was bad. She was going to have to get Susie out of here. The only reason they'd chosen this part of town was because it was one area where Wayman Bishop's influence didn't extend. No, this part of town was under the sway of gangs and poverty, and not even the advisor to the mayor, with all of his power and pull, had figured out a way to bring it under his control.

"As I said before, I'm working on a story," Lily said.

"I hope it's worth risking your life."

"I'll be careful. I always am. Besides, those guys aren't any more dangerous than a roomful of senators."

To her surprise, Mel laughed out loud. The sound of his laughter worked like a talisman against the men at the end of the block. They quickly withdrew, disappearing into the shadows.

"You have a point there, Lily. But where senators may ruin your career, those guys might kill you."

To her surprise, she found herself staring into his dark eyes. It was a second that felt like an instant electric charge—and an eternity. She saw things in those eyes—a flicker of pain and caring, and keen intelligence. It was so sudden and so unexpected, she forgot to breathe.

"That would be a real loss," Mel added softly.

The unexpected compliment in his words made Lily draw in a sharp breath. "I have to go," she said, suddenly more aware than she wanted to be of how handsome Mel was. This tall, athletic man kept himself in shape. He also normally kept himself at a distance, which was part of his appeal. He was good to look at and had been completely unapproachable—until this moment.

"Go home," Mel admonished her. "Whatever your story, it can wait until morning."

"Absolutely," she said, hurrying to get back inside her car. The wind had picked up and she found she was shaking. She rolled the window down a crack. "Please quit following me."

"I've got to head back to the office," Mel said. "I'm trusting you to have the good sense to get out of this part of town."

"Thanks for the advice, Detective." Lily started her car and drove away at a brisk clip. She turned right at the next main road and headed back toward the safer parts of the city. Mel's lights were behind her for several minutes, and then he turned away. Gradually she slowed. And stopped.

For fifteen minutes she waited to see if he'd suddenly appear behind her. But he didn't. He really was gone. Backtracking, she headed toward Cedar Street and Susie.

This time she watched the rearview mirror. She couldn't afford to let Mel discover where she was going. He was already suspicious of her. Now she had to move Susie—and fast.

MEL GAVE UP the idea of tailing Lily again. She was too smart a lady for that. He drove home, wondering exactly what her role in the baby story was. At first he'd been bluffing, but the longer he'd talked with her the more certain he'd become that she was involved with baby David.

But how?

He'd read her newspaper stories. She wasn't a sentimentalist. Just the opposite. She was one tough cookie.

He pulled into his drive and slowly went into his house. He'd bought it a few years before, an investment in a town where real estate was better than high-tech stocks, and a lot safer.

The emptiness of the house hit him every time he opened the front door. No matter how much furniture he bought—the bright throw pillows, the warm and inviting sofas and chairs—the house seemed empty. One reason he worked so many long hours was that he didn't particularly like going home.

He considered cooking something for dinner—a very late dinner, as it happened. It was, actually, closer to breakfast. Instead, he went into the bedroom and started to undress. His mind was on Lily Markey.

He remembered the first time he'd seen her—at a double homicide where a member of the president's cabinet had killed his wife and then himself. It had been a bloody, sad scene, and Lily had hung tough with all the boys. But he'd seen the horror deep in her green eyes. And he'd somehow sensed it wasn't the blood she found so awful, but the waste.

During the past year, he'd run across her at different events. She'd been at the capitol when he'd testified about the need for more money in the public schools for parenting classes. She'd done a good job on the story and had even called him for a quote the next day.

She'd also been in the precinct house a time or two, checking facts. He realized, with a start, that he had a vivid memory of every single time he'd seen Lily. Well, with her auburn hair and sizzling green eyes, she wasn't a woman that a man would forget. He grinned to himself as he remembered the wolf whistles and comments that followed in her wake whenever she left. Boy, that would really make her angry.

And the idea of her anger made his smile widen. She had a temper. Was it her coloring or her convictions? That was a question he would like to find the answer to.

After he found the mother of the abandoned baby.

Lily knew something about that. He wasn't sure what, but something. He could almost smell it on her. Somehow, he knew it was linked with her work. So what would high-level politics and an abandoned baby have to do with one another?

As he stretched out to try and sleep, he knew it would be a night of unanswered questions and little rest. But it wasn't all bad, spending the night with Lily Markey. At that thought, he felt a sudden desire. Yeah, there were a lot worse ways to spend an evening.

"EVERYTHING'S FINE," Lily reassured Susie Bishop. She put the groceries on the Formica table in the tiny kitchen and immediately began to open a can of chicken and rice soup. "I want you to eat, okay?"

"I was worried," Susie admitted. "You were gone so long."

"I had to run by the office," Lily told her. "My boss caught me." She decided against mentioning Mel Haskin. Susie was already frightened enough. It had taken her weeks to win Susie's trust, long hours of conversation and personal revelations. It was only when Susie really believed that Lily understood the emotional quicksand of abuse that Susie had finally trusted "a reporter." Working in Lily's favor had also been the fact that Susie had no one else to turn to.

"Did you check on David?"

Lily hesitated. Was it better to answer the questions about the baby or simply say she didn't know? Susie had given up the child. At least physically. What was the best way to help her emotionally accept that the baby was now someone else's child?

"He's fine." Lily knew she didn't have the heart not to answer. She carried the soup and crackers in to

Susie. "Eat this and then we're up and walking. We need to leave here fast."

"Where will we go?" Susie's eyes widened, a clear blue fear.

"Some place safer. There were some men on the street. They frightened me. I don't like the idea of you being here alone. And it isn't safe for Patti to come and go, either."

Susie looked down into the bowl of soup. "A lot of people are risking serious injury to help me. Why?"

Lily realized she didn't have a real answer to that question. Why was she doing this? Risking her life and her career? "Because it's what should be done," she said simply. "There are good people in the world, Susie. People who want to do the right thing because it is right."

"I thought for sure Wayman had either bought everyone or had them hurt so badly they stayed hidden."

Lily knew it was a quote she'd use in her story. So many lucky people—men and women with safe lives—didn't understand how a woman could put up with abuse. They didn't understand the systematic destruction of all safety nets until a woman—or a child—believed there was no one powerful enough to help them escape. They were all alone. Susie, even now, didn't believe she was safe. Lily had a terrible thought—would Susie ever believe she was safe? Would she ever have the peace of knowing that the sacrifice of her son had been the only choice, for both of their survivals?

"Don't worry about Wayman. In just a few hours, you'll be far out of his reach."

"And David? He's safe, isn't he?"

Lily nodded at the soup bowl. "If you'll eat, I'll tell you." She sat on the edge of the bed. "The Johnsons have already spoken with Judge Patterson. There will be a hearing Monday, and I'm sure the Johnsons will be awarded temporary custody of the baby. Once that happens, then it's pretty much a done deal. David will have a wonderful, safe home. In a matter of weeks, no one will even question where he came from. He'll be safe for the rest of his life."

It wasn't all true. A lot of it, in fact, was the picture Lily wanted to paint. It was what Susie needed to hear to have the strength to keep going.

"He's such a beautiful baby." Susie lowered the soup bowl and brushed the tears from her face. "He'll grow up to be happy and handsome and with every opportunity I could never give him."

"He will," Lily agreed. "Because you loved him enough to save him."

Susie nodded. "And now we have to go." She put the bowl on the bedside table and swung her legs down to the floor. "I'm ready to walk. We have to get going. What about my passport?"

Lily could only admire the other woman's courage. "I should have it for you by tomorrow afternoon. The flight's already booked in your fake name. We just have to find a safe place until tomorrow." She had a sudden thought. "We can go to my place."

"That might not be smart. You're already in this

deep enough. If Wayman ever found out I was at your home, he really would kill you.'' Susie eased to her feet, her face grimacing from the pain. She wobbled a moment, but steadied herself and stood erect. ''That's not so bad.''

''Look. It's less than twenty-four hours before your flight leaves. We can manage to keep you safe and hidden for that long, and I think this place is a lot more dangerous than hiding out at my house for a few hours.'' She had a few concerns, but mostly she wanted to get off Cedar Street and away from the sense of doom that hung over the place.

She clicked on the small television. She'd missed the evening news, but there was a local station that carried a midnight cap of events in the city.

She instantly regretted her decision when the first image that flashed on the screen was a close-up of Wayman Bishop. He was looking down at something, and the camera pulled back to reveal a body covered by a sheet.

''My God.'' Susie's voice was terrified, and just before she collapsed, Lily grabbed her and settled her onto the bed. Both women stared at the television in fascination as the camera closed in on the reporter.

''Mayor Torrell's advisor Wayman Bishop is on the scene. He's checking out the murder firsthand and has a statement from the mayor,'' the reporter said.

She held the microphone out to Wayman.

''Mayor Torrell abhors this senseless violence against women, and the mayor is going to make it his number-one priority to begin the systematic prosecution of men who prey on the women of this city.'' He pointed to the discreetly covered corpse. ''This woman is a victim, and she will be vindicated.''

Lily snapped off the television, but she knew the damage was done.

''What's he up to?'' Susie asked, her voice loaded with fear.

''It doesn't matter,'' Lily said, forcing her voice to sound strong and assured. ''By this time tomorrow, you'll be safe in England. That's all you have to think about.''

Chapter Four

So, the daffodils are blooming, a sure sign that Jack Frost is on the run. Clotilde tells me that Rose was up at the crack of dawn and on the Internet ordering a special baby outfit for little David to wear to court Monday. Special delivery, since none of the shops were open Sunday morning. That baby is going to be spoiled rotten. But Clotilde has a point. What if Rose and Preston aren't allowed to keep the little boy? Heartbreak won't begin to describe what will happen to them.

It's a sticky wicket, as a British kitty would say. But the Internet is a good idea—at least for checking out the maker of that basket.

I've been doing my research, and there's a cute little boutique not far from the Smithsonian that specializes in exactly that kind of basket. Clotilde and I have a date this morning to go there and do a little snooping around. Of course the shop is closed, which is perfect for me. I don't want to buy anything, I just want to look at the books.

I'm wondering how Clotilde is going to take to

breaking and entering, sneaking rides on public transit, dodging humanoids who either want to adopt us or have the pound pick us up—all the myriad facts of my life as a P.I. which she's been protected from.

I can't explain it to Clotilde, but I'm having some trouble with this case. She wants me to find David's mother and make sure that she's not going to snatch little David back. I'm just not so sure I want to find this woman. I mean what kind of mother would toss her kid? Maybe it would be best if we just let her disappear.

See, Clotilde has led a charmed life. Her parents were owned and loved by a wonderful old couple in midtown. When she and her brothers and sisters were born, it was a blessed event. Every single little kitten was wanted. And the humanoids made sure that each kitty was given a loving home.

That's not how it works for a lot of cats. Even now, after years of living with Peter and Eleanor, it's still painful for me to think about my youth.

I never really knew my father. My mother was a beautiful calico. As most cat-lovers know, calico cats are always female. From the day she was born, her humanoids hated her. They didn't want another female kitty. They didn't want kittens, and they didn't want to take the trouble to take her to the vet and get her spayed. So as soon as she was old enough to eat solid foot, they put her in a car and drove to a bad part of town and threw her out in an alley.

They never even named her, but she named herself. Tash. Short for Succotash, that Indian dish of mixed vegetables. She was like that—a mixture of black and white and orange—beautiful. Little and dainty. But life in an alley is hard, and pretty soon, she found herself in the family way.

When I was born, I had two sisters, but they didn't live. There wasn't enough food, and they weren't as strong as I was. I don't know how Mom managed to keep herself and me fed for those first few weeks. I was just getting old enough to hunt for food and forage in the garbage cans when Mom didn't come home one night.

I found her the next day. She'd been run over. They didn't even bother to move her out of the street.

That was the day I left the alley and decided to find a better part of town to live in. I'd been watching humanoids come and go. I followed a car with people dressed in expensive clothes and ended up in a neighborhood not too far from here. I must say, the quality of the garbage was definitely superior. But it was also harder to get to.

At first I thought someone would want me, but they didn't. They'd throw rocks at me for getting in the garbage or trying to catch a bird. I guess because they had plenty to eat, they never considered that I was hungry.

Anyway, to make a long story short, I was nabbed to be an animal used for experiments. I thought that alley was hell until I discovered what humans could do to an animal in the name of science. That's when the microfilm was implanted in me, and I became a pawn in a game I didn't understand. I escaped and met Eleanor, and she met Peter, and as the old saying goes, the rest is history.

Well, enough about the past. Thinking about it doesn't change the facts. I lucked out and found the best bipeds on the face of the earth to love me. And I have Clotilde. Now I have to do this thing that she's asked of me. I only hope I can protect her from the facts of the real world for unwanted cats and dogs.

It's time to head for that little shop, so I now have to go spring Clotilde from her house, which shouldn't be all that hard since Rose and Preston are so absorbed with the baby. Something good has come of this—Clotilde will have a bit more freedom and a lot more time for amoré with yours truly.

MEL PACED the sidewalk in front of Annie's Boutique, waiting for Annie Anlage to arrive and open the shop. He hadn't been completely truthful to the shop owner—she'd bought his story of an abandoned baby hook, line and sinker. Only he hadn't told her that he intended to prosecute the mother for abandonment. He'd led her to believe he was trying to find the mother to make sure she was okay.

He heard the clack of high heels and turned to meet the petite woman who breathlessly opened the door of the shop and ushered him inside.

Out of the corner of his eye, Mel caught sight of two cats slipping through the door, too. If they were her cats, he was surprised she let them out on the street. Traffic was generally heavy around this part of town and untended animals didn't stand a chance of survival. He was about to mention the cats when Annie waved her hand around the shop.

"Which basket? Can you find one similar? Maybe I'll remember who bought it. They're all handmade and I generally remember my clients."

Mel took a breath. He'd never imagined there could be so many different shapes, designs, colors and intricate patterns of woven materials. Some were bamboo, others reed, some vine, some seemed to be paper or fabric. They were all exquisite.

"It was a big basket. Like a baby thing. You know, a carrier, with a handle."

"A bassinet?" Annie asked, smiling at him. "You don't have children, do you, Detective?"

"No ma'am." He didn't bother to add that it wasn't likely he ever would. He didn't have enough faith that he could do a child justice.

"Let me see." She led him to a section of the store that contained larger, more elaborate baskets.

"Like that one," he said, relieved to see one similar to the one baby David had been left in.

"The Bullrushes model," Annie said, her voice filled with amusement. "I only made six of those this year. It shouldn't be too hard to find out who bought them."

Mel examined the basket, surreptitiously bumping the price tag. His eyes widened. It was nearly four hundred dollars. For a basket!

Annie was already on her way to the desk where she began flipping through invoices. "You have to keep in mind that a lot of times the baskets are bought for gifts. The person who paid for it may have given it away.''

She gave a little cry of success. ''Here's the last one. Yes, it was bought about two weeks ago by—it was a cash purchase.'' Her brow furrowed and Mel suddenly felt the lead grow cold.

''Is there a name?''

''I almost always write the name and address. The baskets are guaranteed. It's part of my policy.'' She flipped through several more pages. ''You know, I remember this purchase. The woman was adamant that she wouldn't leave a name. It was very peculiar, like she thought I'd sell her information to some kind of list.''

Or discover that she was planning to dump her baby, Mel thought, but he kept his mouth shut.

''She was a striking woman. Redheaded with huge green eyes. She said it was a gift for someone.''

Mel noticed the black cat sitting behind a huge basket full of peacock feathers. The cat was listening as if he understood every word.

''I gather this woman wasn't pregnant?'' Mel asked. The image of a tall redhead burned into his brain. She kept showing up in the middle of baby stories. Lily Markey.

''No, she wasn't. I mean if she was, she wasn't showing. She was a slender, athletic woman. Tall, very striking. I had the impression that I'd seen her before and when I asked her about it, she got all huffy.'' She shook her head. ''Let me look up the other purchases.''

In a moment she had the list for five names, complete with addresses and telephone numbers. Mel instantly discounted two of the names because he knew the women—and he'd seen them with their new babies. Annie's Boutique was obviously one shop where the women behind the men of Washington shopped.

"Thank you, Ms. Anlage," he said. "You've been very helpful."

"I just hope the mother is okay. You know, all of the women who come in here are so excited about their babies. I used to work in a department store, and some of the women who came in to buy baby things acted like they were going to prison. I—"

"Thanks for your help," Mel said. He hurried out of the shop. He knew the kind of women Annie Anlage was talking about. He knew them well. His mother had been one, and as soon as she could dump her responsibility, she'd done so.

The lead he'd obtained wasn't conclusively connected to Lily Markey. After all, there were thousands of slender, redheaded women with green eyes in Washington. But it was passing strange that wherever he turned in this case, Lily kept popping up. Maybe it was time to pay a visit to her place.

OKAY, CLOTILDE, now's the time for kitty action. I heard everything Mel Haskin heard, and I watched his mind click to the same conclusion. Of course, he was slightly behind me, because cats are simply smarter than Homo sapiens. But he got to the end of the puzzle, nonetheless. Which means I need to re-evaluate all the data regarding baby David.

Lily Markey is involved in this. I can't be positive, but I think she might have been the delivery girl. I do know she isn't the baby's mother. So who is? Maybe her sister? A friend? Someone she works with? How did she become involved in such a scheme?

There's a phone book and now I have to find Lily's address. For a kitty who's only traveled in the back seat of a Rolls, Clotilde is going to learn the wonders of public transit today.

Time's a wastin'. Here's the address, 1414 Union Street. I know exactly where that is.

Dodge, Clotilde! Ms. Anlage has spotted you and she's making those noises that humanoids make when they see something adorable. Watch out, my princess, or you're going to be adopted. I've got the door, let's make a break for freedom.

LILY EXAMINED the passport with a growing sense of satisfaction. It wasn't even nine in the morning and the ball of freedom for Susie Bishop was already rolling. She had a fake passport under the name Sue Bristol, and she was headed for Heathrow Airport in London, where she would be met by an old friend of Lily's, a woman who could help Susie build a new life.

"I'm afraid," Susie said, looking at the passport in Lily's hands. "Wayman will have someone at the airport watching for me. He knows I'm going to try and escape."

"I don't think he'll expect you to go to Europe," Lily said.

"You're probably right about that." But Susie's voice belied the words she spoke. "Do you think we could call and check on David?"

It was the question Lily had been dreading. "I think it would be best if we didn't."

"You could say you were working on a story. I don't want to talk to the Johnsons. I just want…"

"I know, Susie. You just want to make the connection, to know again that David is safe." How was she ever going to help Susie let go of the child? "He is. I'm sure of it. And you have to be too."

"I didn't think it would be so hard." She brushed fresh tears away. "How can I do this?"

Lily went to her and put her hands on her shoulders. "How can you not? What would happen if you went and got David? Where would you go? A single woman, you have a chance of escaping. Your husband will be looking for a pregnant woman or a woman with a child." She didn't bother to point out that Susie was going to have a hard time keeping herself together in a new life. The baby was far better off with the Johnsons. Susie knew it, too.

"Everything you say is true. It's just that—this isn't right."

"Your other option is to press charges against your husband." It was something they'd already discussed.

"And find myself declared an unfit mother. Or dead."

Susie had made no bones about the fact that Wayman could destroy her reputation or even have her killed, and in such a way that he'd never be prosecuted for the crime. He had that kind of power. Susie wasn't exaggerating.

"Your flight is at four." Lily picked up the paperwork. "It's all arranged. You'll be fine. I know it."

She almost dropped the sheaf of papers when she heard the knock on the door. It was so unexpected. She jumped to her feet as Susie scurried into the bedroom.

"Who's there?" Lily asked.

"Mel Haskin."

She closed her eyes to give herself a few seconds to think. What was he doing at her door? And what was she going to do? Quickly she tucked the passport and paperwork into a drawer. "I'm coming."

She glanced around the room to make certain that no sign of Susie had been left in the room, then she opened the door.

"This better be good," she warned him. She was caught unaware by the excitement she suddenly felt as their eyes connected.

"I'm curious about some things," Mel said, striking a casual pose against the doorway.

"I'm busy," she replied. "Maybe later on in the week I'll have time for your curiosity." She started to close the door, but his hand halted her.

"You purchased a basket from Annie's Boutique. A very nice basket. Strangely enough, exactly like the basket that the baby was left at the Johnson house in."

Lily did everything she could to hide the sudden

fear that swept over her. She'd paid cash for the basket. Susie had insisted on buying it—David had to be left in something wonderful, something that would let his new parents understand he was a special child, a wanted child. Now Lily regretted that she hadn't held firm in her objections. But it was too late for hindsight.

"Don't bother denying it. The boutique owner positively identified you."

"Bully for her," Lily said, taking the tack of tough reporter.

"Lily, I don't think I have to tell you that you're playing a dangerous game."

Lily suddenly remembered that Susie could overhear every word they said. She stepped into the hallway. She almost tripped over a black cat that shot through the open door and into her apartment.

"Hey!" she yelled, as a second cat darted inside.

"Those look exactly like the cats from the Johnsons. And the boutique." Mel craned his head around Lily for a better view. "I'll help you catch them." He started inside.

Lily slammed the door shut behind her. "They're mine. Leave them alone."

Mel's brow was furrowed. "I could swear those are the same cats."

Lily gave him a long look. "So cats are following you around, are they? That gives a lot of credence to your detective work."

"Are you denying you bought the basket?"

"I bought *a* basket. A gift for a friend. So what about it? Is there a law against buying baskets?" She stepped closer and caught the scent of his cologne. "I think you're about to step across the line, Detective Haskin. You've obviously got it in for me for some reason, and you're trying real hard to tie me into something that I'm not involved in."

"Oh, you're involved. I just don't know how." He stared directly into her eyes.

"Let me ask you something. I saw that baby. He was well tended. He's been taken in by a family who wants him. Why are you so determined to make a case out of this?"

Mel didn't answer instantly. His gaze held hers, and for a moment she thought she saw a flicker of pain. Then it was gone, replaced by a hardness that made her want to step away from him.

"I don't like women who shirk their responsibilities by dumping babies on doorsteps."

"That's a mighty big assumption on your part."

"Not so big. The baby was abandoned. It was left like a ham or a basket of tomatoes—something that someone *might* want. But there were no guarantees. What if no one had gone out on that veranda for a day or two? The baby would have starved to death."

"No, it wouldn't. Someone would have found it."

"How can you be so sure?" Mel persisted.

Lily was tempted to say because she was watching from the top of the stone wall, that she would never have left the baby without being positive he was safe. She couldn't say that, though. She shrugged.

"The baby was found. He's wanted. He'll have a

perfect home. Why isn't that enough for you? If the Johnsons want him, why can't you leave it alone?''

"Because a crime has been committed. A crime against a helpless infant. And part of my job is protecting the helpless.''

Lily considered that for just a few seconds. ''Who are you trying to punish, Detective? Your mother?'' She saw instantly that she'd scored a direct hit—and it had done nothing to help win him over to her side. If anything, she'd only made him angrier.

''This isn't about me. Just take heed of this. Whoever dumped that baby is going to pay with jail time. I promise you that.''

He turned and walked away, his broad shoulders squared and his head high in anger.

Chapter Five

Mel had got control of his temper by the time he reached his car. Behind the wheel, he sat for a moment and forced himself to think. Why did Lily Markey get under his skin so? Normally, he didn't take his cases personally. But something about Lily brought his emotions right up front.

He found her attractive. There was no denying that. But there were thousands—hundreds of thousands— of good-looking women in the city. There was something else about her. As her image flitted through his mind, he realized what made Lily so unforgettable. He'd seen that spark of passion in her eyes, and he recognized it.

She believed as deeply in her work as he did his. She went after a story with everything she had, yet she never forgot she was writing about people. She wasn't after the headline—she was after the truth.

That was part of it—that commitment to principle and ideal. But what kind of principle allowed a woman to get involved with a scheme to abandon a baby? She might be passionate and idealistic, but somewhere along the line her ideals had gotten scrambled.

He drove toward the precinct. There was a chance Lily would follow through on her threat and report him for harassment. With that in mind, he knew he had to file a report. He'd been acting without official approval—always dangerous for a law-enforcement official. As soon as his report was read, though, he knew he'd catch hell for pursuing the case. After all, abandoned babies were the province of Human Resources or Social Services, not homicide detectives.

So, his part in the case was just about done anyway. Lily and her secrets would have to be pursued by someone else.

At his desk, he focused his thoughts on the baby and wrote his report. Lately he'd become a very proficient typist. But he stumbled several times. After a moment's hesitation, he noted Lily's role in the case. He made no direct links or references, but he did remark on her presence at the Johnson home and her link to the baby basket.

He spared a thankful thought for the wonder of computers as he spell-checked his report and shot it into the system for his boss to read first thing Monday morning.

Still at odds with his emotions, Mel headed for a late Sunday breakfast at Emerald's Café, one of his favorite places on a blustery spring morning. Outside the café, he picked up a Sunday paper and with a cup of hot coffee in front of him, found himself searching the paper for Lily's byline.

To his surprise, there were no stories with her name on them. He couldn't remember a day when she hadn't uncovered some political dirt. He closed the paper and felt the tightening in his gut that told him a hunch was on the way. That's when he saw the flagged stories at the top of the front page.

Lily had no bylines, but her picture was featured inside a box with a promotion for her upcoming series on spousal abuse.

There was a quote from her that made his gut tighten further. "My research indicates that the women of Washington are under-served—no, completely unserved by our system. From the poorest of homes to the estates of the wealthy, women are beaten, intimidated and abused."

"Tell me it's not so," Mel said softly to himself as he studied the paper. He read the quote again. So Lily was out of politics—or at least, the politics of the Capitol—and into the politics of gender. Who was *served*, who wasn't. For a fact Mel knew that domestic abuse took a back seat in law enforcement. Officers grew jaded with women who, jaws and limbs broken, refused to press charges or testify against their husbands. It was a catch-22. They were afraid to testify and afraid to complain, because they ran the risk of more brutality, or even death, if their complaints didn't stick.

The end result of Lily's story would be that the heat would be turned up on law enforcement, especially after the murder of a woman and Mayor Torrell's interest in "protecting the women of Washington."

Mel pushed the paper aside, finished his coffee and decided against breakfast. His instincts were working, and the best place for them to work was while he was jogging. Maybe afterward he'd eat something and take a nap.

LILY STOWED the suitcase in the trunk of her car. She went back into her apartment and checked Susie's hastily purchased attire. The navy business suit was nondescript, and wearing it, along with the navy pumps, navy bag and blond wig, Susie no longer looked like the frightened wife of a powerful man. The bruises were covered with makeup and the sophisticated lines of designer clothes had been traded for the off-the-rack anonymity that would be necessary for Susie to get out of town.

"I don't know if I can do this," Susie said, turning to stare at her reflection in the hall mirror.

"You have to," Lily said matter-of-factly. "I'll be with you the entire way, until you board the plane."

"I just…" She took a ragged breath.

Lily went to her and grasped her shoulders firmly. "You've come too far with this to back down now. What are your options, Susie? We've been through this a thousand times."

"I know." She pulled her shoulders back. "Sometimes I think back five years, to when I first married Wayman. He treated me like a queen when we were dating. He sent roses every day. He brought me gifts and seemed to enjoy my friends. We had cook-outs and dinner parties."

Lily saw the stunned look on Susie's face in the mirror. She couldn't imagine marrying a man only to discover that everything he'd shown had been a façade, a lie designed to lure her into a trap.

"He's not a part of your life anymore," Lily reminded her. "You're going to have a new life, a new identity. You can find happiness, Susie. My friends will help you."

"Sometimes I just think that maybe I'm crazy. That maybe I've made up all the beatings and cruelties."

"Have you checked your medical records lately? I have. Two broken wrists, a fractured tibia, both cheekbones cracked, a broken nose, numerous broken ribs. Do you think you dreamed all of that?"

Susie shook her head. "How did this happen to me? I didn't come from a home where people hit each other. I went to college. I was smart. I had a career. When I met Wayman, I was second in the chain of command at an advertising agency. I was making great money. I had a terrific apartment and a good circle of friends. Bit by bit, Wayman forced me to let go of all those things. First the apartment, then the job…and then my friends. He found fault with every one of them, once we were married.

"The worst part is that I let him. I tried to resist, for a while. I saw my friends secretly, meeting for lunch. I guess that was the first time he hit me, when he caught me having lunch with Doris. So I gradually stopped answering the phone. I lost contact with everyone who might have helped me. How did that happen?"

"I don't know," Lily answered softly. "The scary part is that it could happen to any woman walking the face of the Earth. But it didn't happen to you because you deserved it, Susie. You can't ever believe that."

"I think the thing that scares me most is that if I let it happen to me once, it might happen again. What if I give up my baby, move to England and start over only to discover that I need the kind of man who hits me?"

Lily didn't have any answers. She simply hugged Susie. "My friends will help you. You'll see. I don't think you'll ever let another person, male or female, abuse you again. I have that much faith in you." She squeezed her shoulders again. "Now we have to go. I want to get to the airport early to check things out."

Susie bent and picked up two of her bags. "Thank you, Lily. I know what you're risking, and I can never make you understand how courageous you are."

"Nonsense," Lily answered briskly. "Let's go." She paused in the living room, eyeing the two cats. Both had curled up on the sofa as if they belonged to her. She recognized the cats, too. They'd been at the Johnson's house.

The fact that they'd somehow traveled across town—with Mel Haskin?—was a puzzle she didn't have time to contemplate at the moment. When she got home, she'd call the Johnsons and arrange to return the kitties. That would give her one more excuse to check up on the baby.

She opened the door, and before she could stop them, both cats leaped into action and shot out the door and down the hall. They disappeared around the corner.

"I'll be," she said to Susie. "Did you see that?"

"They aren't your cats?"

Lily shook her head. "I have no idea who they actually belong to. I can only say they seem to know how to travel around this city better than most humans."

Susie laughed. "A cat negotiating public transit? That's a good one."

"Yeah, isn't it?" Lily said, laughing too. She picked up the remaining suitcases and the two women loaded the car and drove away.

NOW I'VE GOT a clear picture of what's going on in this case. It's a lot more complex than I ever thought. Clotilde, too, has grasped the situation. Little David isn't unwanted—poor Susie is giving him up to protect him. I suppose my initial assessment of her was a little harsh.

So, Clotilde wants to know, what should we do?

Go home and make sure little David is safe. Something tells me that Wayman Bishop hasn't dropped the idea of finding his wife and baby. He's going to tear this town apart, district by district. Thank goodness Lily is getting her out of the country. Susie might actually have a chance for a life without abuse and fear.

And David? That's Clotilde's big concern. It doesn't sound as if Susie wants to give him away. Will she come back later and claim him? That's a question beyond the ken of even Familiar, Feline Detective.

Clotilde is worried. Each day that passes, Rose and Preston will grow to love that little boy more and more. If Susie decides to come back and get her child, it will devastate them. So what is a black feline to do?

I don't know. I honestly don't know. I just want to get back to the Johnson house and make sure everything is okay there. I don't like the way my elegant black fur bristles when I think of the Johnsons. It's almost as if my kitty intuition is telling me that something bad is about to come down.

MEL FOUND THAT not even a five-mile jog had settled the anxiety in his gut. Normally a good run put everything in perspective, but not this time. He showered, dressed and found himself in his car, driving through the manicured neighborhood where Preston and Rose Johnson lived.

He didn't intend to disturb the couple. There was something fishy about the baby, but he didn't believe it came from the Johnsons. He'd always prided himself on being able to recognize good people, like the Johnsons. They were as wholesome as American apple pie. He'd be willing to stake his career on it.

So why was he driving around their house as if he thought they might be hosting a counterfeit ring? Because something was going to happen. He knew it as surely as he knew his name.

He drove slowly by the house, and it looked like a photograph for a garden magazine. All seemed in order. He cruised on down the street, wondering why he felt as if he were about to jump out of his skin.

DUCK, CLOTILDE, it's the long arm of the law! What in the world is Mel Haskin doing cruising my neighborhood? At least he didn't stop. I'm telling you, that man is going to be serious trouble in the long run.

I want Clotilde to go on inside. I'm going to survey the exterior. I just have a bad feeling. There goes my pretty little kitty, right through the open door by the library. Safely home once again.

Well, she didn't have to slam the door in my face. And was that the lock I heard clicking into place?

I'm going to—hey! What's going on? That guy is wearing a mask! And he has a gun—pointed straight at Rose Johnson. Hey! Damn it! Who locked the door?

LILY KEPT one eye on Susie while the other watched the airport. Dulles was never slow, but on Sundays it seemed the lines for international flights were somewhat shorter. Susie huddled in a blue chair, ticket safely in hand. She was already checked in, having passed the identification process with flying colors. She hadn't even flinched as she pronounced her new name. Lily allowed herself a feeling of success.

It was nearly three o'clock. Soon the plane would be boarding. Lily could feel the tension in her neck and shoulders. She was a bundle of nerves. Wayman Bishop was a powerful man. He could make *her* disappear. She'd known that fact before she agreed to help Susie. Now, though, as they neared the finish line, Lily was more aware than ever of the risk they both took.

But it was nearly over.

Lily glanced at Susie once again. Susie seemed absorbed in watching the local news on one of the overhead televisions.

Lily saw the horror register on Susie's face first. Then she heard the piercing scream. Nearly tripping over her own feet in her haste to get to Susie, Lily bounded across the terminal.

"What?" she asked, grabbing Susie's shoulders.

Susie pointed mutely to the television.

The footage was ragged and bumpy, but Lily instantly recognized the Johnson house. The photographer was obviously running with the camera as he tried to follow a police officer who moved quickly in a crouched position directly toward the Johnsons' front door. The officer had his pistol drawn. In the background, half a dozen officers huddled in various positions of assault.

Mel Haskin stood right in the middle, his face drawn in worry as he lifted a bullhorn to his mouth.

"We have the house surrounded. Give yourself up and come out!"

The only answer was a series of rapid gunshots.

Chapter Six

"Clotilde!"

The creep is shooting at my lady!

"Run, Clotilde! Under the sofa!"

I've got to get inside the house. I hope my sleek fur is tough, because I'm going through this window!

"Eee-yow!"

The crash and my wild cry got the masked gunman's attention. I'm inside now, dodging through the glass. There's his thigh. If I can get a grip on it, I'll be too close for him to shoot, unless he wants to hit his own leg.

Now I've got him. The savage use of teeth and claws is extremely gratifying. He's dancing on one leg, but I'm hooked in like a burr. Take that, you beast. Ah, blood. I'll tear him limb from limb.

"No, Clotilde, stay safe."

She's on his other leg like the little tigress that she is. My lord, she's a vicious feline.

"Jump!" *Now to make it to safety. Under the sofa again. And he's on the run! There he goes across the yard. The cops are shooting at him. They can't seem to hit him. Dang, he's over the wall and gone.*

But Clotilde is safe. Now to check on Rose and the baby!

MEL DASHED THROUGH the front door, tumbled and rolled to his feet, gun drawn. The house was too quiet. He feared the worst until he heard the soft sobbing from the parlor. Waving the backup policemen into the house, he darted into the parlor. Rose Johnson sat on the sofa, weeping into her hands. There was no sign of any intruders.

"Mrs. Johnson," he said, rushing forward. "Are you okay?"

"Yes, thanks to Familiar and Clotilde." She lifted her face and pointed to the cats. "They ran him outside."

Mel looked at the open French doors just as two officers burst through them.

"He went over the wall," one said. "Jim and Stan are after him."

"If he gets away..." Mel didn't finish the statement. He didn't have to. "Where's the baby?" he asked.

Rose took a deep breath and slowly regained control. She brushed the tears from her face and sat up straighter. "Preston took him in to see Dr. McAdams." She shook her head. "We wanted David to have a thorough checkup before the court date tomorrow, and Kevin McAdams is a family friend. He agreed to see him in the office today as a special favor to us.''

Mel felt a rush of relief. The baby was safe. He turned his full attention to the crime scene. He noticed the broken windowpane, and finally the black cat who was busy licking his side. The smaller calico cat beside him was nuzzling him.

''The window?'' he said.

''Familiar came through it like a cannonball,'' Rose Johnson said, admiration clear in her voice. ''He saved Clotilde and me. That awful man was shooting at my cat. He said he was going to kill her and then me.'' She sobbed again and struggled for control.

Mel stared at the two cats again. They'd been across town only an hour before. Lily could claim them if she wanted, but he knew different. It was just another odd element of the abandoned baby case—traveling cats. He intended to look into it, just as soon as he had a spare minute.

Mel sat down beside Rose, taking her icy hand in his. ''He's gone now. Try to pull yourself together. If we're going to catch him, we need your help.''

''Of course,'' she said.

''Shall I call your husband?''

''No! No, don't do that. Let him take care of little David. I'm honestly not hurt, just a bit shaken.''

Mel gave her a moment as he waved the other officers to get busy and check the rest of the house.

''There was only one intruder?'' he asked gently.

''Yes, just the one. I was in the nursery. I didn't go to the doctor with Preston and David because I'd called a decorator. I was waiting for him to arrive. I was very foolish. When the doorbell rang, I just opened the door.'' She put her fingers to her lips. ''It was very stupid of me, I know.''

''No one expects an armed gunman to break into their house on Sunday afternoon,'' Mel reassured her. ''Just tell me what happened.''

''As I said, the doorbell rang. I opened it and this man pushed the door so hard I fell down backwards. Then he was in the house.''

Mel wondered at a burglar so bold that he would strike while the house was occupied. The type of person who did such a thing had no regard for human life. Rose Johnson was a lucky woman—her cats had somehow managed to save her. He glanced at the elegant black cat. It should have been impossible, but he'd swear it was the same cat he'd seen across town. He looked more closely and was surprised when one golden eye winked at him. It was almost as if—he pushed the thought aside and concentrated on his interview. ''Did the intruder say anything? It might be helpful if we knew what he was trying to steal.''

''Steal?'' Rose looked at Mel blankly. ''He wasn't a robber. He was here to get the baby.''

''The baby?'' Mel felt the knot of anxiety in his stomach twist even tighter. Somehow, he'd known this was all connected to the baby.

''Yes. The first thing he asked was where the baby was.''

''What did you tell him?'' Mel said, forcing his

voice to remain gentle. Rose could never know how important her answer might be.

"I said, what baby?"

He wanted to kiss her. She had the instincts of a mother, and little David was one lucky kid to have been dumped on her doorstep.

"What happened then?"

"He, uh, well, he grabbed my hair and lifted me up." Rose's eyes filled with tears again, but she held them back. "He said he was going to kill me and take the baby."

"And you said?"

"I told him to search the house, that there wasn't a baby here. I was just so relieved that none of the baby furniture had been delivered. Thank goodness you took the basket and blanket for evidence. There was absolutely no indication that David had been left here."

"Did the intruder search?"

"He held the gun at my spine and made me go with him through the house."

Mel felt a surge of anger that made him lean forward. He didn't want Rose to know how furious he was. He didn't want to do anything to frighten her further. But he knew if he got his hands on the man who'd hurt her, he would take immense pleasure in making him feel pain. "There was no evidence of the baby?"

For the first time she smiled. "None." Her smile faded. "And that made him very angry. He said he knew the baby was here and that he was going to start destroying the things I loved until I told him where he was.''

"Did he use the baby's name?"

Rose thought for a moment. "No. In fact, he called David *it*. Which means he didn't know that the baby I had was a boy."

Mel nodded. "That's interesting." He filed it away. The intruder knew the Johnsons had a baby, but he didn't know the gender. That meant perhaps that he'd seen the infant, or that he knew the mother and wasn't certain of the child's sex. It was a very important clue. Thank goodness, whatever angle Lily was working on with the baby story, she hadn't printed a word of it yet.

Mel saw that Rose was holding herself together by sheer force. A sideboard held a selection of liquor. He got up and poured a small amount of bourbon in a glass. "You probably don't drink your bourbon neat, but sip this. For medicinal purposes."

He admired Rose even more when she accepted the glass and took a swallow. She was a woman with spirit and extraordinary good sense.

"What did the intruder do next?" he prompted.

"We were here, in the parlor, and my cat, Clotilde," she pointed at the calico, "came in through the French doors. He slammed the door and locked it. And then he aimed at Clotilde. He said he was going to kill her unless I told him where the baby was."

"And you refused." It was a statement, not a question. Mel already knew the answer.

"Yes, I denied there was a baby. So he started

shooting. That's when Familiar, the black cat, crashed through the window. He was on the man's leg like a panther.''

''Mrs. Johnson, have those cats been here all day?'' He knew how bizarre his question sounded when Rose Johnson gave him a slow look.

''Yes. All day.''

Mel eyed the two cats. He suddenly saw the red splotches beneath the black cat. The animal was bleeding. He got up and went over to the cats. ''I think maybe we should check out Familiar,'' he said as casually as he could. ''He's bleeding.''

''Oh, my lord,'' Rose said, rushing to the cat. ''Give me the phone. Familiar's owner is a vet, and he lives across the street.''

Mel handed her a portable and in a moment she was talking to someone. She gave brief details and then put the phone down. ''Peter's on his way right now.''

''Meow.'' Familiar nodded.

''How badly is he hurt?'' Rose asked.

Mel wasn't certain he should touch an injured cat—especially one that had the reputation of diving through glass and attacking armed men. Nonetheless he bent down to look at the cat. Even as he probed what looked to be nasty gash in the cat's side, he was rewarded with a purr.

''It's a cut,'' he said, ''not a bullet wound.''

''Thank goodness for that.'' Rose hurried into the kitchen and came back with several clean dishcloths. ''Let's put some pressure on it until Peter gets here.'' Very carefully she lifted Familiar into her arms and pressed the towels against the wound. Clotilde stepped into her lap, licking Familiar's face.

"She knows he saved her life," Rose said, looking directly at Mel.

The logical detective in him wanted to dismiss the remark, but there was something in the way the cats behaved that made him think twice. It was as if they did understand. And the black cat *had* hurled himself into the room. Deliberately. Mel was positive now—these were the same cats he'd seen in Lily Markey's apartment, no matter what Rose Johnson thought. The cats had been across town and back.

"Those are some extraordinary animals," he said.

"Oh, officer, you don't know the half of it," Rose answered just as Peter Curry rushed into the room.

So this is what it's like to be a wounded hero. I could let the humanoids know that it's a cut from jumping through the window, and though it hurts and stings, I'm not in danger of dying. But why spoil their fun? And Clotilde! Lord, she's about to lick my whiskers off. And those little mewling sounds are sweet music to my ears. I feel like John Wayne in a western.

But here comes Peter, and it won't take him but a minute to determine that my life isn't in danger. Then he'll bundle me home and try to make me stay there. I just hope I don't require stitches. Cats really don't like stitches, you know. I suppose there's not a species around that actually wants to be sewn up.

Ah, Peter is examining my wound while all the others look on in concern. Even that detective is looking a little worried. And I thought he was such a hard case. You know, there's more to ol' Mel Haskin than meets the eye.

Peter says I'm going to live. And a good thing, too. I'm too young to croak. And Clotilde would be heartbroken. Uh-oh, he's going to put that stinging medicine on me! Yikes! And I can't try to run or struggle. It would blow my image as a hero. Dang him, Peter is smiling at me. He knows exactly what I'm thinking. He's doctoring me in public so I can't afford to put up a fuss! Well, I'll get even with him later.

Right now, I want to find out what the coppers did with that masked man. I sure hope they caught him. Shooting at my lady! Just let me say that when Familiar finds him, he's going to have a hefty price to pay.

LILY BROKE all speed records leaving the airport and heading toward the Johnson home. In the car beside her, Susie was almost beyond reasoning.

"It's my fault," she kept saying again and again. "I never should have tried to run. I never should have let David out of my arms."

At first Lily had tried reasoning with her, but in the end, she'd given up and decided to concentrate on driving.

"When we get there, you're going to have to drive away," she told Susie. "You can't go inside. You know that."

"I have to see my baby," she wailed.

"No!" Lily's harsh tone stopped the crying. Susie just sniffled.

"Let me go inside and see what happened," Lily said in a gentler voice. "There's a phone here." She pointed to the glove box where she kept her cell phone. "I'll call you as soon as I find out what's happening."

"What if they hurt David?"

"I'm certain he's okay," Lily said, though she wasn't at all certain. What would prompt a daylight attack on the Johnson home? There was only one thing—baby David. Somehow, Wayman Bishop had discovered the whereabouts of an abandoned child and sent someone to grab him. Wayman couldn't be certain that this baby was his son, but he was certain enough to send a henchman to abduct the child. An armed henchman who didn't care how he got his way or who he injured in the process.

She and Susie were on the street where the Johnsons lived, and she slowed the car and pulled to the curb. "Remember, Susie, drive over a couple of blocks and park. I'll call you."

"Okay." Susie slid behind the wheel as Lily got out of the car.

"Can I count on you?" Lily asked, suddenly worried that Susie might do something that would endanger all of them.

Susie nodded. "I'll do what you say. But if Wayman has hurt David," she finally looked up at Lily, "I'm going to kill him. I mean it, Lily. I'll get a gun and I'll shoot him down in the street. I should have done it long ago.''

Lily nodded. "I'll help you. I promise. But David is fine. I'm sure of it." Before Susie could see the chink in her façade, she hurried away.

It was only a couple of blocks to the Johnsons', but the way was littered with members of the press and police officers. Luckily she had her newspaper identification, and she avoided the police and dodged her fellow reporters. The only real answers were inside the house. And she intended to get inside.

At the front door she was stopped by a policeman who refused even to consider her request to speak to Rose Johnson.

"No way, Ms. Markey," he said. "Detective Haskin would have my head."

"Mel Haskin is inside?" Her heart almost exploded with fear. Mel had been on the baby case. The only reason he would be here would be the baby—or a homicide.

"Yes, ma'am," he's in there.

"Tell him it's Lily Markey," she pleaded. "I know this case. I can help him."

The officer hesitated.

"I'll stand right here, and if he doesn't want me to come in, I'll leave without any trouble."

The policeman eyed the other reporters who were watching like wolves for any sign of weakness. "I'll ask him."

He closed the door and Lily paced inside the covered entrance, waiting. When the door opened, she was surprised to see Mel.

"Isn't this a little off your beat?" he asked. "But then again, you've been off your beat for the past few days, haven't you?"

"I'm wondering the same about you." Then she couldn't play the game any longer. "Is the baby okay?"

For a moment she thought he wasn't going to answer her. Then something in his face softened, and she felt the most intense connection with this man she hardly knew.

"He's fine," Mel said. "In fact, he isn't even here."

"Can I come inside? Please?"

She saw him hesitate, and then to her amazement, he opened the door wide enough for her to enter. Before the gathered media could rush the open door, he slammed it and locked it. "I'll have hell to pay for playing favorites, so I'm expecting something in return for this," he said as he escorted her into the parlor. He'd already come up with an idea.

"What might that be?" Lily focused on Rose Johnson, who sat on the sofa with the veterinarian from the evening before. His name was Peter Curry, Lily remembered. They were holding the black cat, with a big white bandage around his abdomen.

Mel's fingers on her arm were light but insistent. "We're going to play this story as a simple home invasion. Robber breaks in with the idea of intimidating a lone female to give up all the valuables. There will be no mention whatsoever of a baby. The media outside only know there was a break-in. Give me your word that you'll play it the same way."

Lily nodded. She had no objection to keeping the focus off the baby. In fact, that was what had to be done. "You have my word. If I write anything, it'll go the way you say."

Mel's hand was still on her arm, a strong hand that she was aware of on several levels. His fingers increased their pressure and the effect was startling. Her breath caught in her throat. She looked directly into his eyes.

"There's one other thing," he said. "I want the truth, Lily. There's something going on here I don't understand, and you know what it is. I want you to tell me before that baby is injured."

MEL KNEW he'd hit a nerve. He could see it in Lily's green eyes. She did know something! And she was guilty as hell about it.

"What happened?" Lily asked, trying to hide her emotions.

"This isn't for print," Mel said. He'd always been leery of trusting the press, but this time he knew Lily had a personal stake in the matter. He was playing a hunch, and the old feeling of trusting his instincts was strong and solid.

He quickly went over the sequence of events, ending with the story of the cat's heroism. "Funny thing, too. Those are the same cats I saw in your apartment this morning," he pointed out. He saw that Lily recognized them, too. He was glad to see that Peter was comforting Rose Johnson. Now he could focus on Lily.

"How did the cats get back here?" she asked.

"I was going to ask you that question."

She shook her head. "That's something I honestly don't know, Detective."

He took her arm and steered her down the hallway and into a library. He closed the door. "The baby is safe. You've got the whole story. Now I want some answers, and you're the only person who can give them to me."

Lily looked around the room. There was no escape, and he pointed to a sofa. "Have a seat, Lily. We're going to talk."

"There's nothing I can tell you," she said simply, taking the seat he indicated.

"Can't tell or won't?"

"A little of both. Would you mind terribly if I used the phone?"

"Yes. I want you to answer some questions first." He could see that his answer made her anxious. What important phone call did she need to make?

"Please, Detective. It won't take but a minute. It's urgent."

"Okay. There's a phone on the table there." He watched as she walked across the room. She was one beautiful woman. Tall, slender, and with a walk like a goddess. She picked up the phone and then turned to look at him.

"I'd like some privacy."

He considered refusing, but decided that it would be in his best interest to step out of the room—as long as he left the door wide-open.

"Sure," he said. "I'll see if Mrs. Johnson can spare us a drink. I think you need one."

"Perfect," Lily said, the receiver already in her hand.

He was barely out the door before he heard her dialing. Pressing himself against the wall, he shamelessly eavesdropped.

"It's me," she said. "The baby is safe. He wasn't even in the house. Just wait for me, okay? Before I leave, I'll give you a call and you can pick me up."

There was a pause while the other person talked.

"No, I swear. David is fine. So are the Johnsons. Everything here is fine. There was an intruder in the house. But don't worry. And just wait for me in the car. I'll call you."

She replaced the receiver and Mel slipped off to the parlor to mix the drink he'd promised. So, someone else was worried about the baby.

And it might possibly be the woman he wanted to find—the mother who'd put David in such a dangerous position by abandoning him.

Chapter Seven

Mel felt a sharp pain in the calf of his leg and looked down to find the black cat, claws of one paw hooked in his pants, staring up at him.

"What?" Mel asked, then looked around to make sure no one heard him talking to the cat. It honestly seemed as if the black creature could read his thoughts. Familiar. It was a perfect name for the animal. He did seem a little supernatural—and a lot witchy—with his golden, knowing eyes.

"Meow!"

There was a distinct accusation in the cat's tone. As if he knew that Mel had eavesdropped on Lily.

"It's my job," he said. "If she has facts pertinent to the baby, I intend to get them. Any way I can." Once again the ridiculous idea that he was talking to the cat made him wince and check to make sure he hadn't been overheard.

The black cat held him with a stare, then slowly turned his head side to side. He was saying no!

"I'm hallucinating," Mel said, shaking his head. He needed a drink more than Lily. He walked past the cat and checked on Rose and the veterinarian. They were deep in conversation, and Rose seemed much calmer. Two uniformed officers were dusting the doorway for prints and another was making notes. The situation was well in hand.

Mel quickly prepared a bourbon and water and a plain ginger ale and headed back to Lily. She was seated on a sofa, waiting for him, the absolute picture of innocence. And beside her, the calico cat purred and rubbed against her hand.

He handed Lily the bourbon and looked directly into her green eyes. They were an odd green—brilliant yet with a hint of golden brown, perhaps even a swirl of teal. Eyes that a man would never forget.

"Why are you staring at me?" Lily asked.

Mel abruptly looked away. His gaze locked with the golden one of the black cat, who had also slipped into the room.

"I'm sorry," Mel managed. "I was…" He couldn't tell her the truth—that he felt as if he'd fallen into the green depths of her eyes. "I was wondering what your big interest in the Johnson family might be. Preston Johnson is a highly respected lawyer, but environmental law normally isn't of interest to a political reporter…or a politician, unless he's running for office," he pointed out.

"And a baby generally isn't exactly the province of a homicide detective."

Lily Markey gave as good as she got—and when she did, her eyes shifted color to a bright kelly green. Mel would be willing to bet, too, that at certain other times sparks jumped in the depths of those crystal irises.

"Well, since the attack on Mrs. Johnson today was *almost* a homicide, I feel the case is getting closer and closer to my *province,* as you so quaintly put it."

He saw the fear that swept across her features, and he almost regretted his bulldozing tactics. Almost. But he had to find out what Lily Markey was doing in the middle of an abandoned baby case. And soon. Because if someone didn't figure out what was happening, there was every possibility he would find himself trying to solve a homicide.

"Did the intruder threaten to harm Mrs. Johnson?" Lily said, her voice restrained.

"First let me ask you—is this because you're a journalist covering a story, or do you have another interest in this case?" Her answer would tell him a whole lot about her motivations—which were beginning to fascinate him more and more.

"You're asking if I want the official version or the truth?" she shot back.

"That's not what I'm asking. What's *your* interest? It looks to me as if it's more personal than professional, and I'm just wondering why. Is it the Johnsons?" He let three beats pass. "Or is it the baby? And that would make me wonder why a Washington political reporter has a tender spot for one particular baby."

He saw her hesitate, and for a split second he thought he might actually get a truthful answer. But when she looked back into his eyes, her green gaze was carefully shuttered.

"I'm working on a story," she said. "I'm not sure this is part of it, but it may be. I can't tell you more than that."

The disappointment he felt was far out of proportion to what it should have been. Just for that instant he'd seen something in Lily that had affected him like…like the ridiculous hope that Santa Claus was real. But it was gone so fast he wasn't certain he'd even seen it. He had to stick to facts, and the fact was that Lily wasn't being honest with him. He sighed. "I have your word none of the details of what happened in this house today will see print?"

He saw that her gaze never wavered, and her answer came instantly. "I gave you my word. I'm good for it."

He nodded. On that he did believe her. Out of the corner of his eye he saw the black cat nod also. The dang animal was agreeing with his deductions!

"Let's get the details right, then," he said, determined to ignore the cat. "An intruder forced his way into the house. He wanted valuables—wasn't there a story on television recently about the Johnsons' collection of historical papers?" At Lily's nod, he continued. "That's perfect. The papers are in a bank vault, and when Mrs. Johnson told him that, he said he was going to kill her. We arrived and the intruder fled."

"Me-ow!" A strident cry broke the flow of his story. The black cat was standing over the smaller calico. With one paw he patted the calico's head.

"What in the world?" Lily said.

"Me-ow!" Familiar demanded again. The calico joined in the yowling complaint.

"I forgot the part where the intruder shot at the calico and the black cat came through a window, attacked the intruder and then ran him out of the house." Mel felt like a fool recounting that part of the story. He knew it sounded as if he believed the cat had actually done such a thing. Sure, the window was broken and Rose Johnson swore that sequence of events had happened exactly like that. But Mel didn't believe in rescue cats, or Santa Claus…or a woman without an agenda.

"Amazing." Lily picked up the black cat and gently settled him onto her lap. She was rewarded with a sandpaper tongue right on her palm. "This is an extraordinary animal." She quickly caught her mistake and reached over to scratch the calico. "And this one, too."

"You honestly believe the cat did such a thing?" Mel was surprised that "never-let-a-story-go" Lily had no difficulty in accepting the cockamamie tale of a rescue cat.

"Of course I do. Cats are highly intelligent, and they can be very loyal when they truly love a human. And these cats obviously love Rose Johnson."

"Meow." Clotilde's cry was softer, sweeter than Familiar's, and it ended on a loud purr.

"I feel I've just fallen through the looking glass," Mel said. When Lily's head snapped up, he shrugged. He saw the look of surprise, then appreciation in her eyes. She didn't have to say a word for him to know her exact thoughts. "So I like to read," he said, embarrassed. "It isn't a crime."

"*Alice in Wonderland?* Most adults have forgotten that book by the time they reach our age. Unless they have children they're reading it to."

"No kids." Mel felt his stomach knot. "I decided a few years ago to read some of the children's classics. I sort of missed them when I was growing up."

He saw the shadow of curiosity in her eyes. She wanted to ask him about his childhood, and he saw her decide against it. He expected to feel relief, but instead he felt a twinge of disappointment.

"As for your trip to Wonderland, Detective Haskin, these cats are pretty remarkable. The black one was wounded, I see. Not a gunshot?"

"No, he cut himself on the window. He's fine, though. His owner is a veterinarian," Mel reassured her.

"I'd say these cats might even be worthy of a story, if—"

"If you were a feature writer." He made his point clearly.

"Yes," she smiled. "If I weren't a political reporter. Which brings us back to this attack. What do you think the intruder really wanted? What, exactly, did he say?"

Mel knew instantly that she wanted to believe that the man who might have killed Rose Johnson wanted only valuables. Lily had a stake in the safety of baby David. He was positive of it. His gut instincts told him he was dead-on. Now the question was, how did he play it?

"Don't act dumb, Lily. You know this wasn't a home invasion or some robbery attempt." All expression left her face. "Someone was after that abandoned baby. Someone with a gun who intended to do whatever he had to do to get baby David back."

"Could..." Lily's voice broke and she cleared her throat. "Was Rose able to identify the assailant?"

"He wore a mask."

"Did he say anything that might give a clue as to why he would want this baby?"

Mel saw the fear in her eyes, and he felt compassion for her. She was sincerely worried. He realized with a twist of strong feeling that this wasn't just another story for Lily—as it wasn't just another case for him.

"He didn't know the gender of the baby. All he knew was that the Johnsons had a new infant in the house. He wanted it. He told Rose that if she didn't give him the baby, he would start killing things she loved. That's when he shot at the cat."

"Oh my." Lily's shoulders sank in defeat. Then hope appeared again. "Your men, they're going to catch him, aren't they?"

Mel clenched one fist. "I don't know. He went over that back wall and disappeared. I'm sure he had an accomplice, someone waiting to pick him up."

Lily stood and put her almost untouched drink back into his hand. "I need to speak to Rose, and then I should be going."

"Not to the newspaper." Mel made it a statement, but it was more a question.

"Not to the paper. I gave you my word."

"You said this story *might* figure into something you were working on. What could that be—the illegitimate baby of some powerhouse politician who has suddenly decided to claim his heir?"

Mel was surprised at the startled look on Lily's face.

"Actually, my story is about women, not politicians." She shrugged her shoulders in an attempt at innocence that almost worked. "Women who find themselves in situations of abuse where there aren't any good solutions."

All of Mel's tender feelings instantly vanished. "You wouldn't be implying that there might be a good reason some woman would abandon her newborn baby, would you?"

Instead of defeat, Lily's face registered a stubborn passion. "Yes, I would be saying that. Surely after all your years on the street, you've seen situations where a woman might not have another choice—for the safety of her child and herself."

"What I've seen on the streets is more along the lines of women who don't want to shoulder the responsibility of a child. Children get in the way of lifestyle—whether it's top-of-the-heap social events or the neighborhood beer bash. Having to put a child first makes a life of pleasure a bit harder. And I don't have any tolerance for women—or men—who create a child and then toss it off at the nearest doorstep because it might interfere with their fun."

Lily's eyes were wide with surprise. Mel, too, was surprised at the passion he'd displayed. Surprised and annoyed. He knew better than to let his personal feelings out in front of a reporter. Damn it. Lily had tricked him. That was probably how she got all her great stories—those big eyes—and even bigger ears. Hell, he should have frisked her for a hidden tape recorder.

"Detective, you asked me what my interest in this case was. I ask you the same question."

There was heat in her voice—anger. Mel understood it fully. "Let's just say that I deal with a lot of unpleasant people—murderers, thugs, addicts and the like. They inflict a lot of harm on themselves and each other, which I try to prevent, or at least hold someone accountable for. I'd like to stop all that behavior, but I can't. So I've accepted the fact that adults inflict pain on each other. But I won't tolerate an innocent child being abused. And no matter how you try to pretty it up with explanations, abandonment is abuse. Horrific abuse."

"Why are you so..." Lily broke off the question. She shook her head. "Maybe one day you'll be able to see that women aren't always given good choices. Maybe one day you might understand that sometimes love forces a mother to find an alternative destiny for her child—even when it breaks her heart to do so."

"I seriously doubt that day will ever come." Mel stood up. "I have to get to work." He stalked out of the room and left Lily to find her own way out of the house.

As soon as Mel was gone, Lily hurried to the telephone and called her cell phone. Susie picked it up on the first ring.

"Tell me he's fine."

"I told you before, he's fine. Pick me up four blocks west of here, okay?"

"I'll be there."

Lily replaced the phone and hurried to the room where Rose Johnson was talking with her neighbor, the handsome veterinarian Peter Curry. Mel Haskin was nowhere in sight. Now was the time for her to make her exit.

"Mrs. Johnson, if you learn anything about the intruder, would you give me a call?" she asked.

"Yes," Rose answered. "I will. I know this story will be covered by the media. I respect your work, Lily, and your integrity."

"Thanks. I'd better be going." Lily beat a retreat before anyone else got curious about her sudden interest in the Johnson family.

She hurried out into the fading afternoon light. Her emotions were in turmoil. She'd almost committed the unforgivable. For one instant, she'd felt as if she might be able to trust Mel Haskin with the truth. She'd wanted to tell him. God, she'd wanted to confess it all and let him help her.

But there was no guarantee Mel would help. In fact, the exact opposite was more likely. All she had to do was remember her sister, Babs, lying in a hospital bed with both cheekbones broken, three teeth cracked and a total of a hundred and forty-seven stitches in her scalp—all compliments of her then husband, Officer Bobby Reynolds.

And when Babs had tried to press charges—had tried to get the system to protect her—not a single officer had come to her assistance. No one wanted to go against "a brother in blue," as they said.

The one lesson Lily had learned from the situation was that police officers stuck together no matter what. She couldn't afford to trust Mel with the truth. It had almost cost her sister her life—and she wasn't risking Susie.

No, she'd have to solve this new set of problems on her own. When the chips were down, she could count only on herself. It just kept things simpler if she remembered that fact. She sighed as she thought of the latest tangle in her efforts.

Susie had missed her escape to London, and baby David was in danger. Those were hard, cold facts. Her plan to help Susie and the baby had backfired. So what was she going to do now?

There was no easy answer to that question.

Making sure that none of the officers and reporters still milling about on the Johnson lawn were paying attention to her, she started walking down the sidewalk toward her rendezvous with Susie. The best thing they could do was get out of the neighborhood and figure out a new course of action. She knew without a doubt that Susie Bishop would never leave Washington now.

The solution that had been within her grasp only a few hours before was gone. And the danger had increased a hundredfold. Wayman Bishop knew about the baby. She was certain of that. The man who'd attacked Rose Johnson was Wayman's henchman. She didn't have to have fingerprints to prove it.

She turned a corner and found Susie sitting behind the wheel of the Mustang convertible she'd bought five years before. It was a car made for sunny drives through the country—a luxury she seldom had but often daydreamed about.

She hurried to the car and opened the door. Just as she was about to slip inside, she had the strangest sensation that someone was watching her. She scanned the street in both directions. A sedan was parked far down the block, but it appeared to be empty. It was hard to tell with the tinted windows.

"What is it?" Susie demanded. "Is someone following you?"

Lily shook her head and settled into the car. A black shadow darted out from behind a maple tree, startling Lily to the point that she almost screamed. The cat leaped into the back seat.

"He scared me nearly to death," Susie said, her hand at her heart. "Tell me, Lily. Is everything okay?"

"David is fine," Lily reassured her. "Get us out of here. The place is crawling with cops, and I'm afraid some of them are reporting directly back to your husband."

Susie took her at her word and hit the gas pedal so hard the tires squealed as they spun out down the road.

"What are we going to do? I have to get my baby." Susie was gripping the wheel so tightly her knuckles were white. "I was wrong to let him go. That man, he was shooting. He meant to kill someone."

"I don't think so," Lily said, though she wasn't at all certain that if David had been home, Rose and Preston Johnson might not be dead at this very moment. "He was after the baby. I think he fired the shots to frighten Mrs. Johnson. He was aiming at her cat." She glanced back at the handsome black cat, and wondered where he'd left the beautiful calico. They were very peculiar cats.

Susie drove toward a main highway, pausing finally. "Where should we go?"

That was the question of the day. Lily was afraid to go back to her apartment with Susie. If Wayman knew about the baby and the Johnsons then he very likely knew about her role in Susie's escape from him. While the murder of the Johnsons might cause a stir, Lily had the sour thought that a whole lot of folks in Washington—especially the politicians she'd dogged— might not be too upset if she disappeared.

And no one would search for Susie.

She felt a tiny prick on her left shoulder and turned to find the black cat staring at her. His mouth held a sheet of paper.

"What?" She was so amazed she took the paper, which was clearly what the cat intended. It was a flyer for a new restaurant on the Potomac. One that specialized in fresh seafood.

She looked at the cat for a moment. "Drive us to the river," Lily said, hardly believing she was saying it.

"The river?" Susie was confused and still afraid.

"The cat wants to go there."

Susie cast a glance into the back seat. "The cat?"

"Meow," Familiar said, purring and rubbing his head on her shoulder. "Meow."

"Let's get something to eat," Lily said. "The cat's right. We need some food and we need to think."

"Couldn't we find a place closer to here?" Susie asked. "I don't want to leave the area. I want to stay near David."

Very gently Lily put a hand over hers on the steering wheel. "We can't stay here, Susie. You know that. Wayman is watching this area. I'm positive of it, and you are, too, if you'll admit it. For your sake, and David's, we can't hang around here. Let's go to the river." She reached back and scratched Familiar's head. "I'm not certain, but I think the cat is trying to tell us something, and at this point, I'm willing to listen to anything he has to say."

"Our destiny is in the hands of a cat?" Susie demanded, her fear flaring.

"This isn't an ordinary cat," Lily assured her. "Let me tell you what happened at the Johnsons'. This cat is a hero. Now just drive and listen."

THE MAN WITH THE CAMERA slipped quickly into the shrubbery bordering the road. Mel sat in his patrol car and watched through binoculars. The photographer aimed his camera at Lily. There was another woman in the car, driving. Mel didn't recognize her.

He'd intended to follow Lily and see what she was

up to. Now he was torn. The photographer made him curious. Lily was well worth a photograph, but why would someone be…stalking her? He focused the binoculars back on the shrub. The media would do anything to get a story, but this guy acted suspiciously. Very suspiciously. And Lily wasn't a story, she wrote them.

He could see the camera lens protruding from the shrubbery, still aimed at the Mustang and the two women. Mel made a decision. He could find Lily if he had to. Right now, he wanted the identity of the cameraman and an explanation for his behavior.

Chapter Eight

Miss Pulitzer needs a guardian angel, especially one that's sleek, black, highly intelligent and has four paws. I'd prefer a cushy job with a little easy armchair watching, but I'm afraid this time I'm going to have to stay extra alert. I've deduced that my newspaper gal and her friend are in grave danger. I know Mel will leave officers to guard the Johnsons and little David, but no one is keeping an eye on Lily and Susie. And since Lily isn't hard to look at, I'll volunteer.

Clotilde was a little annoyed that I made her stay home, but once I pointed out that her humanoids need protection, she agreed with great good spirit. That Clotilde, she is the best. Loyal, loving, magnificently attractive and all mine.

I couldn't help but listen to the little conversation between Mel and Lily. I don't know how astute Lily is on picking up clues to the male psyche, but ol' Mel was giving out some pretty good hints. His interest in baby David is personal, and very deep. Abandonment is an issue with him. And like most of the males of the humanoid species, I'm afraid he's going to be pig-headed about listening to another side of the issue.

I'm pretty sure I've got all the facts put together, and the way I see it, Susie Bishop acted in the best interests of her child. A very selfless action, I might point out. Now, making Mel see it that way is going to be the hard part.

For the moment, though, I've steered my bevy of beauties—actually I don't think two qualifies as a bevy—my duo of dames toward the Potomac and a restaurant with quality seafood and a great view. There's also a houseboat there, which belongs to Peter and Eleanor. Ah, I remember my first encounter along that very waterway—back when I was a stray and those vile men had implanted microfilm under my hide. I solved my first case and Peter and Eleanor saved me, and gave me a home. I'm hoping the river will prove as lucky for Susie and Lily.

Here we go. So far I don't see a tail following us, but I did see that man with the camera. He wasn't out shooting pictures of birds. No, Lily and Susie are in danger. I'll just have to keep them safe.

LILY REACHED FOR the cell phone on the second ring. She was surprised to hear her sister's voice. Babs had just been on her mind.

"I left three messages at the newspaper. What's going on?" Babs asked.

Lily hesitated. No one would sympathize with her plight more than Babs, but she didn't want her sister to worry. Babs knew better than anyone how dangerous it could be to try to escape an abusive husband.

"Just busy working," Lily said.

"I spoke with your boss. He's looking for you, too. This isn't like you, Lily. No one is more dedicated to her job. Tell me the truth, what's going on?"

"Honestly, Babs, just work. I'm busy and I haven't checked in regularly."

"I'm coming to Washington. I can hear in your voice that something is wrong."

"No!" The one thing Lily didn't want was to reopen the old wounds that Babs had finally begun to recover from. Involving her in a case like Susie's would be highly traumatic.

"That's it. I'm catching the train. I'll be at your apartment tonight. You'd better be there or I'll…"

"I'll call you tonight and talk with you. Just stay put. Promise?"

"You'd better call," Babs warned her. "I'm worried about you."

"I'll call." Lily replaced the phone and glanced at Susie.

"I'm sorry, Lily. I've dragged you into such a mess."

"Not to worry. Look, there's the turn-off to the marina. Let's see where this cat wants us to go." She reached into the back seat and gave Familiar a scratch. "He's extraordinary, don't you think?"

"He certainly gets around," Susie agreed. "How can we check on my baby?"

Lily sighed. "I'm working on it. I can't go back to

the Johnsons. At least, not right away. But I think I have an idea. This cat belongs to their neighbors. Maybe I can call them and tell them I have him and then ask about baby David.''

Susie's face showed her relief. She turned the car into the marina area and slowed.

"There. Fisherman's Wharf, finest seafood in the city.''

"Me-ow!'' Familiar put both front paws on the car seat. "Me-ow.''

"I think he's hungry,'' Susie said.

"Well, let's give him anything he wants. He saved the day, Susie. It's time for a reward.''

MEL SAT in the unmarked patrol car and watched Lily being driven away. What was her connection to the baby? He recognized Lily's car, but he'd run the tags just to be sure. He didn't recognize the woman who'd been driving, but he knew instinctively that she was deeply involved in baby David's life. Lily and her friend were in it up to their ears. And he wasn't the only person who knew it.

The man with the camera slowly eased out of the shrubbery. He looked up and down the street, then began walking away at a brisk pace. Mel was out of the car in a flash.

"Hey! Police, halt!'' He called the words even as he reached for his gun.

The first bullet that whizzed past him was close enough for him to feel it. The second almost caught him, but he ducked and rolled.

The man not only had a camera but a gun with a silencer. Mel came out of the roll on his feet, gun drawn. He couldn't shoot without endangering civilians. It was an exclusive neighborhood with large, wooded yards, but houses were everywhere. He didn't have a clear shot.

"Damn!" Mel took off as the man darted through a backyard.

Mel pulled out his radio and called for backup, then continued his pursuit with all of the strength and endurance of a man who jogged and worked out on a daily basis.

He wasn't surprised to discover that the man he pursued was also in top physical shape. Mel gave no ground as he darted over the expensive brick walls and through carefully landscaped lawns, but he didn't gain on his quarry, either. His radio crackled as his men joined in the chase.

He paused long enough to bark into the radio, "How the hell can these suspects keep escaping us? I want this guy, and I want him able to talk. Send a unit over to Cherry Lane to cut him off. Get a helicopter if you have to. Whatever it takes. I want him brought in!"

To Mel's surprise, his quarry changed directions, angling away from Cherry Lane where police forces were gathering to apprehend him. It was almost as if he—and the man who'd attacked the Johnsons—knew exactly what moves the police were making even as they made them. Impossible!

He had a cold knot in his stomach at the thought of

why a man with a gun and a camera might be photographing the area. His gut told him Lily or the other woman in the car were the intended targets.

Lily! Why couldn't she simply tell him the truth? What had she gotten herself into?

His worries almost betrayed him. He saw the mysterious photographer stop and take aim just in time to dart behind a gazebo. While Mel knew he couldn't risk shooting, the gunman had no such compunction. He obviously didn't care if his bullet went into a home and killed an innocent bystander.

Mel scrambled to his feet with renewed energy. He vaulted a bench and gained on his opponent, cutting him off and heading him back toward Cherry Lane. If the backup unit was in place, they'd have him!

Mel slowed and punched his radio. "He's headed right for you. Fan out and take him."

The words were barely out of his mouth when the gunman cut right, then another hard right. He was headed back in the direction he'd originally come from! As if he knew the police were waiting!

Mel was stunned. Now there was no one to help stop the man. He had to do it himself. He poured on the speed and saw the gunman stumble. He went down hard but regained his feet and disappeared behind a cabana beside a huge, aqua swimming pool. Mel followed. He slowed only when he saw the camera lying on the ground. The strap was broken, obviously by the hard fall.

He left it, knowing he could come back for it, and continued the chase. He was only fifty yards behind when he saw the gunman slow at Plum Avenue. A sleek black car, windows tinted, pulled to a stop, and the passenger door opened. The gunman dove into the car. Tires squealed, and the car roared down the street.

Mel had time to notice that the license plate had been covered. There were no other distinguishing marks on the car. He gritted his teeth. There were probably thousands of black cars like that in Washington.

He got on the radio and called for pursuit of the car, but, in his heart, he knew that once again the quarry had escaped.

Panting, he went back to retrieve the camera. He lifted it gingerly by the strap. With any luck, there would be fingerprints on it. He hadn't caught a good look at the gunman, but he had seen the man's hands had been bare.

Although Mel was disappointed that the gunman had escaped, he didn't have time to dwell on it. He had to check out the neighborhood and be certain that no civilians had been injured in the gunfire. And he wanted to spend some time reviewing the sequence of events.

First the break-in at the Johnsons—and that gunman's clean getaway. Secondly, the escape of the photographer/gunman. It was possibly the same man, but Mel doubted it—at least, he hoped not. How could a man who was the object of an intensive police search avoid being captured by hiding in a shrub?

And how had both gunmen evaded the police so easily?

Mel knew the answer, and he also knew he didn't want to confront it. The intruder and the cameraman had access to police information. They'd somehow been able to pick up the restricted line Mel had been using to talk to his men. Someone in uniform was helping them. Mel let his anger burn away the residue of bitter disappointment he felt. The code of loyalty among police officers was legendary. There was no creature lower than a policeman who jeopardized his fellow officers. But somewhere among the men he knew and worked with, there was a snake.

And Lily was the object of the gunman's interest. Mel began to pace. He had a mental picture of her driving away, her beautiful red hair blowing in the wind. She'd been completely unaware that someone was photographing her.

Mel studied the expensive camera. It was the kind a professional would use, and could possibly lead to the man who'd dropped it. But it was the film Mel really wanted, and he intended to personally deliver it to the lab to have it processed and the camera checked for prints.

Within a few hours, he'd have some answers!

"WHAT'S WITH THE CAT?" Susie asked as she watched Familiar jump onto the houseboat.

"I'm not certain." Lily knew the cat was trying to tell her something. She'd completely accepted the fact that Familiar was extremely unusual. He'd made his menu selection abundantly clear—fried crab claws as an appetizer, grilled shrimp and a side order of crabmeat au gratin. The cat had eaten as if he'd never seen food before in his life.

She watched as Familiar paced the deck of the houseboat and then disappeared. In a moment he returned, and she could clearly see the key hanging from a ring in his mouth.

"I think he wants us to stay on the houseboat," Lily said, wondering if she'd lost her mind.

"You've got to be kidding." Susie, too, was skeptical.

"What else could it mean? He has the key."

"It could mean the cat wants us arrested," Susie said, but her voice lacked conviction. "What are we going to do?"

Lily didn't have to give it much thought. They had no place to go. Sure, they could check into a hotel, but Wayman Bishop had a network that was so extensive, she didn't trust anyone. By now, he would have put out the word that Susie was alive and hiding from him. Her picture would be circulated among every lowlife who owed Wayman a favor. And Lily had no doubt the stool pigeon would be well rewarded for turning Susie in.

"We're going onto that houseboat."

"It belongs to someone with money." Susie was still hesitant. "I mean look at it. It's a beauty."

"Familiar has a lot of wealthy friends," Lily said. She was surprised to hear the humor in her voice. But it was true. The cat hung out with some mighty ritzy folks. "This must belong to someone he knows."

"Me-ow!"

"See," Lily said. "He agrees." She stepped off the dock and onto the boat, adjusting her balance to the very slight shift of the boat in the water. "Come on, Susie. This is the best place we could be. No one will ever think to look for us here."

"Meow!"

The black cat did a figure eight though her legs as she held out a hand to Susie and helped her board.

"Me-ow!" Familiar demanded.

"Let's see what he wants," Lily suggested. Without waiting for Susie to agree, she followed the black cat into the galley. She found the light switch and discovered the houseboat was ready for occupancy. The kitchen was lovely—blue and yellow tile creating a cheerful place.

"Meow." Familiar jumped onto the counter. His black paw patted a tile and Lily walked closer to inspect.

"To Eleanor, with all my heart. Peter."

One of the tiles had been hand-painted. Lily's fingers brushed the cool ceramic surface. How long had it been since she'd allowed herself to believe in true love between a man and a woman? Far too often marriage had seemed like a business arrangement to her—with the woman in the position of clerical staff while the man was CEO.

But there were good relationships. There had to be.

"What is it?" Susie asked.

"A fairy tale," Lily answered. She stepped away from the tile. No point making Susie feel worse than ever by pointing out that Eleanor, at least, had found a good man. Or so it seemed. After a moment of real pleasure at the prospect of such a wonderful marriage, Lily felt the hard shell of her skepticism settle over her. Peter and Eleanor's relationship might look good from the outside, but there was no judging what it was really like. That was what she had to keep in mind— to prevent such Pollyanna thoughts.

Better safe than sorry, that was the lesson she'd learned from her sister Babs.

MEL WENT THROUGH the photographs one more time. He'd memorized them, but he still looked again. The shots of Lily were clear, showing her in all her willowy grace. Her red hair was gently tossed by the April breeze, and her short skirt showed off her long legs to advantage. She was one helluva woman, by any standards.

He focused on the other woman. She wore sunglasses, and her face was partially concealed by long blond hair. She, too, was attractive, but she didn't hold a candle to Lily. Of course, that was simply because Lily epitomized his ideal woman—smart, stylish, beautiful, determined.

And pigheaded to a fault.

So what did the photographs mean? They were shots typically made by a private investigator, usually in a domestic situation. The sort of photographs that showed someone doing something immoral, illegal or both. But Lily wasn't doing anything wrong. And as a high-profile reporter, her face was on camera and seen at hundreds of events. It wasn't like she was some reclusive celebrity.

So it had to be the other woman. He signaled two other detectives over, men he'd worked with for years. From now on, he'd have to be careful who he trusted. "Can we identify this woman?"

"Why don't you ask Lily Markey? That's her in the pictures. She should know who she's with."

"Good point. I somehow don't think Ms. Markey would tell me the truth, though."

The men looked at the photograph. "Hard to say, but we'll get on it."

"That's what I wanted to hear." He turned his attention to the telephone. In a moment he had the Washington, D.C., Police Department crime lab on the line.

"Have you got the results on the prints from the camera?"

There was a pause. "We've made a match," the technician said. "Positive ID on Jim Lavert, one of ours."

Mel hoped he'd misunderstood the technician's inference. "One of ours?"

"Yeah, on security detail to the mayor. Special assignment. You've got his folder up there, I'm sure. All of those men were hand-picked."

"Thanks." Mel replaced the phone. Though it was late in the day—a Sunday, no less—the place was busy. Detectives and officers conferred over desks and in corners. Suspects came in and out of the interrogation rooms. But Mel felt strangely alone.

Jim Lavert. He knew the man, yet Lavert had fired on him—and not just warning shots. The man had intended to kill him.

He picked up the photographs. It was time to take what he had to his chief. This case had gotten deep—and dirty.

No wonder the photographer/gunman had known every move the police were making. It would have been so simple for him to tap into their radio frequency. Lavert knew all the trade secrets. He'd worked as a homicide detective in another precinct before going to work with the mayor.

Mel closed the door and put the file in front of his boss, Lester Bennett. ''I want Jim Lavert brought in for questioning. He shot at me today, and he fired recklessly in a residential neighborhood.''

''Lavert?'' Bennett was shocked. ''He's been on the force for fifteen years. Are you sure it was him?''

''Positive prints on the camera.''

Bennett nodded, though his face was drawn into a frown. ''This isn't going to look good on the force. You know that.''

''I know it.''

''Could someone have set Lavert up?''

Mel considered it—for about twenty seconds. ''He was the man with the camera and the gun. He fired on me, and he wasn't sending warning shots. He was also photographing Lily Markey. So if you think this is bad now, just imagine what it's going to be like if Lavert does something to a newspaper reporter.''

"I'll call the mayor right now. I hate to bother him at home—"

"Bother him," Mel said. "This has gone too far, Lester. Home attacks, neighborhood shootings in one of the best neighborhoods in the city—it's completely out of hand. I don't know what's going on, but I think Jim Lavert may be able to give us some answers. And I want them before someone is killed."

Chapter Nine

Lily and Susie are all tucked in on the houseboat. I'm sure Eleanor and Peter won't mind, but I promised Clotilde I'd meet her by midnight.

I'm worried about my lady love. As much as the Johnsons want that little baby boy, I don't want to see anyone hurt, especially not Clotilde. It took at least three of my lives today when I saw that maniac shooting at her. He intended to kill her just to make a point. I don't think I've ever felt so helpless. And now I'm torn between watching over Clotilde, who is, at least compared to the humanoids, far more capable of avoiding disaster, and watching these women.

I can stand guard, but I can't prevent Susie's husband from doing something heinous. No one can. Unless I somehow convince Mel that he has to help Lily and Susie. Then I'll have to convince Lily that she can trust Mel. Bipeds! They've lost their basic instincts and they muddle around in irrational behavior.

I watched Lily look at the tile that Peter had painted for Eleanor and installed on the boat as a special surprise. At first, Lily was charmed by it. Then I saw her face harden. She's an anti-romantic. Which means that she's incredibly romantic and has been hurt. In humanoids, every force is a reaction to a counter-force. Find someone who can't abide smoking, scratch the surface and there's generally an ex-smoker there. Action-reaction. Bipeds are rather knee-jerk about everything, and most especially about love. One experience and they establish their reaction to tender feelings. They don't have a clue that it's their expectations which bring about many of their experiences.

Take me, for example. I expect the ladies to find me sexy, suave, keenly intelligent and a kitty they can't resist. And I've never been wrong. Name me one case where the lady in question didn't want to take me home and keep me. It's true. I expect to be worshipped, and so it happens.

Find a woman, or a man, who disavows true love and you'll find someone who's loved wholeheartedly—and been hurt. That's Lily in a nutshell. If I could figure out what happened in the past, I might be able to make some inroads. But I don't have a lot of time to work on Lily's injured psyche. I'm too busy trying to save her hide.

Susie's story I know. Powerful, abusive husband. And from what chitchat I've picked up at various Washington social functions, I know Wayman Bishop won't give up searching for Susie until he finds her—or her body. And he's never going to let that baby go. I just wonder how he found out baby David was his offspring.

What I need to do is check in with Clotilde and, first

thing tomorrow, have a sit-down with Mel. Easier said than done. Although I can understand feline and humanoid language, Mel only speaks English. I do believe America should become bilingual. Every human should be forced to learn the language of at least one other species, preferably feline.

If humanoids took the time to try to understand a cat, or a blue jay, or a horse, the world would be a very different place. Even a slobbering, subservient dog could teach them a few things, such as loyalty and unconditional love. Of course, I don't believe humans should learn too much of the dog-type worship. Unrestrained, they're a very destructive species.

Oh, well, it's a long trip back to Mulberry Road. It's going to take some creative "hitching" to find the ride home that I need. Time to get cracking.

LILY LISTENED to the soft sounds of Susie's rhythmic breathing. Susie had fallen asleep instantly, her body exhausted by the rigors of childbirth and the constant stress of her situation. Lily shifted positions, wishing she could fall asleep. She was worn to a frazzle, but her mind wouldn't stop.

"Dad-blast-it," she said, sitting up. She'd forgotten to call her sister. Babs would be on her way to Washington, D.C., if Lily didn't stop her.

At the thought of what her sister had endured—and overcome—Lily felt a bit of satisfaction. It had taken five years of counseling and three operations to repair the damage Bobby had wreaked on Babs. But now her sister was the CEO of a small design company, and

she was living a life that was both interesting and re-
warding.

Five years before, Babs had been a puddle of fear,
anxiety and self-loathing. All because Bobby was the
kind of man who felt big by making a woman feel
small.

Lily slipped from the bed and went up on the deck
of the boat. She took her cell phone and found a comfortable spot on deck to place the long-distance call.
She punched in the numbers and listened to the rings.

On the third, Babs picked up.

"I thought I was going to have to come and check
on you," Lily's big sister said.

"I'm fine. Just a complicated story." That wasn't
exactly a lie. "How are you?"

"Better than you'd ever expect." Babs laughed
softly. "I've met someone, Lily. Someone wonderful."

Lily felt as if an arctic wind had blown out of the
clear sky. "What?"

"I've met a man. He's terrific. Kind, gentle, caring.
He's a novelist. I want you to meet him."

There was no room in Lily's mind to imagine
Babs's new man—her mind was too filled with images
of her sister's bloody face, the broken cheekbones, the
smashed ear, the bandages all ready to wrap her broken ribs.

"Lily? Are you there?"

"Yes." She carefully controlled her voice. She
wanted to ask if Babs hadn't learned her lesson the

first time around. Bobby had been the man of her dreams—until he exchanged compliments for his fists.

"I know this frightens you, Lily. I understand that what happened with Bobby was harder on you than it was on me because you had to watch it happen and couldn't stop it. I was so deep in it I couldn't see, thank goodness. But Luke isn't like that. He isn't."

"Are you sure?"

"As sure as I can be. But I want you to meet him. Form your own opinion."

"My opinion won't matter a bit," Lily said, her fear and anger showing in her voice. "I thought Bobby was a slick-talking con man, and *you* thought I was nuts."

"I've learned a lot about myself in the last few years." Babs's voice was calm, gentle. "I've changed, Lily. I'm not the same woman who allowed her husband to abuse her. If I can't believe in the power of change, then what's the use?"

That was a valid question. Lily knew her sister had worked hard to change herself, to learn how to reach for a better life.

"Just promise me you won't do anything rash."

"Those days are over. But Luke and I want to come down next weekend. Is that good for you?"

"By then, I hope to have my present situation resolved," Lily said, making her voice mocking and light. "If it isn't, you might have to visit me in jail."

"You must really be on to something juicy," Babs said. "Just be careful. You know, as much as you worry about me, I worry about you in equal measure. I worry that you won't let any man into your life, and that you work all the time, and that you put yourself in danger. Whether it's a husband or trying to nail a criminal, danger isn't a good place to be.''

Lily couldn't deny the truth of Babs's words. Her sister had learned a lot. ''I love you, Sis. I'll look forward to meeting Luke.''

''I love you, too, baby sister.''

Lily punched the telephone off and leaned back against the cabin of the boat. The night was filled with stars and the gentle sound of the water. The houseboat was a place designed for romance. Peter Curry and his wife had probably shared some wonderful moments together on it.

Lily's thoughts drifted to Mel Haskin. She was attracted to him. She was honest enough with herself to admit it. But she was also afraid of him. He was a law officer, a man who was used to wielding his authority. And he had the power to hurt Susie.

If the situation were different, Lily wondered if she might actually pursue her interest in Mel. It didn't matter, because right now she couldn't afford such thoughts. Too much was at risk. With his attitude toward baby David's mother, Mel was nothing short of the enemy. For all of her words of warning to her sister, she had to keep that thought firmly in mind.

MEL AWOKE WITH A START. His hand reached across the bed, finding only emptiness. At the feel of the cool sheets, he finally gathered his thoughts and realized that Lily was not in his bed. It had all been a dream. All except for his desire to have her.

He threw back the covers and walked, naked, through his house. There was no point in trying to go back to sleep. The dream of Lily had been so intense, he knew he would not be able to relax again.

In the kitchen he put a pot of coffee on and checked the time. Nearly five o'clock. Monday morning. While he could do nothing about his fantasies regarding Lily, he could take action against Jim Lavert. By now the beat officers should have him in custody. That was the order Mel had left—put him in lockup and leave him overnight.

A few hours in the holding cells with drunks, drug addicts, thieves and other assorted criminals ought to do a lot to loosen the tongue of a man, especially a man who was a member of law enforcement.

Mel knew that his boss wasn't keen about the idea of arresting an officer and putting him in a holding cell. But Mel had insisted, and based on the evidence against Lavert, Les Bennett had gone along with the idea. A little hardship now might save the police a lot of work on down the line.

With his first cup of coffee in hand, Mel retrieved the morning paper and sat down to read it. He looked for Lily's byline and was disappointed not to find a story by her.

Lily. She was in his thoughts even when he wasn't aware of it. Lately, though, he'd been all too aware. He decided to forgo breakfast, took a quick shower and headed out. He went to Lily's apartment.

When he realized she wasn't home, he felt a twinge of concern and then relief. Lily wasn't stupid. Whatever she was involved in, she was smart enough not to lead anyone to her place. She was hiding. He knew it, and he was glad. Of course, with his resources, he could find her.

And the other woman. It was time to solve that mystery. She was the key to Lily and to baby David. He'd awakened with some solid feelings, if intuition could ever be called solid. "Feelings" wouldn't hold up in court, but Mel had learned to trust his. The random hunches that he got were what made him a better than average lawman.

That other woman in the photograph was the mother of baby David. He knew it as surely as he knew his name. Lily was involved in the abandonment. He couldn't believe that she'd actively take part in leaving a baby on a doorstep, but she was helping the mother. Why, he didn't know. But he was going to find out— in a matter of a few hours. And then he could begin to build his case.

Even though it was only seven o'clock, Mel drove to the precinct. As soon as he walked in the door, he knew something was wrong. Tension telegraphed itself throughout the building. When he saw Lester Bennett at his desk so early, he knew whatever it was was serious.

Lester motioned him into his office, and Mel was surprised to discover two men in expensive, tailored suits already there.

"Mel, these gentlemen are part of the mayor's private security force." There was just enough sarcasm in Lester Bennett's tone to let Mel know the lay of the land. Les was highly annoyed. Highly!

"What, the mayor declared a holiday today?" Mel asked. "No one told me."

The two men were not amused. "One of the mayor's most valued employees is missing. We understand you might have something to do with his disappearance," one man said.

"Yeah, I work as David Copperfield's assistant on the side." He saw the warning look his boss shot him. "Who's missing?"

"Jim Lavert." The man let the name drop like a stone into the silence of the room. "I believe you know him. I also believe you were looking for him."

"Not me personally," Mel said slowly. He didn't like the way the deck was stacking against him. It was almost as if the two suits were accusing him of foul play. "Some police officers were looking for Lavert at my request, that's true." He gave no more information and saw Lester's minute nod of approval.

"Why were you looking for Mr. Lavert?"

"I believe that would be *Officer* Lavert?" Mel couldn't help himself. The suits got under his skin. "Though he was assigned to protect the mayor, he is an employee of the Washington, D.C., Police Department." He kept his tone level, but he made his point with force. "I'm sorry, gentleman, I didn't catch your names before you started hurling questions and innuendoes." He was furious, but he knew he had to keep control of his temper.

"Staples and Crenshaw," the same man said.

"Catchy names," Mel said. "Sounds like a comedy act." He saw his boss roll his eyes and wanted to smile but restrained himself.

"Look, Mr. Haskin—"

"*Detective* Haskin," Mel pointed out. "Let's keep this conversation on a formal level. Very formal. So that if there's any hint of impropriety, we'll be able to nip it in the bud."

"Look, Detective Haskin," the man said with deliberate patience, "the mayor wants to know where Laver...*Officer* Lavert is. If you know something, now would be a good time to tell us. This is very important to the mayor. And I'm sure you and your boss don't want to unduly upset Mayor Torrell in any way, especially by a lack of cooperation."

"Well, boys, I was actually hoping Officer Lavert would be right here in this building this morning. I had some questions to ask him." Mel looked at Lester Bennett.

"We had several officers looking for him last night. He didn't return home, and no one has seen him. I might add that his wife is extremely upset," Lester said.

Mel kept his expression neutral, though he found the news more than a little disturbing. Lavert must have figured out that he'd been identified and had fled. With his inside knowledge of how the police system worked, Lavert was going to be a hard man to run to ground.

"Have you got his place staked out?" Mel asked.

Lester nodded. "Phone lines are tapped."

"Why are you so interested in Officer Lavert?" one of the men in suits asked suddenly. "Did he do something?"

Mel started to answer but hesitated. That was something his boss should handle. Lester had a sense of politics that Mel lacked.

"We have some questions for the officer about a case he was working on," Les said smoothly.

"He wasn't working cases. He was assigned to the mayor's security."

"True enough," Les said with ease, "but he was also picking up a little extra cash on the side doing some surveillance and things like that. It's possible he might have seen something related to a case we're investigating. If he did, I'm sure he'll be more than glad to cooperate. Jim Lavert has a flawless record with this department."

Lester delivered his speech and then stood, indicating that the meeting was over. "Thank you, gentlemen. If we find the officer, we'll be sure and give you a call. It's likely that he's simply pursuing one of his cases. I'm sure he'll be in touch with his family sometime today."

The two suits stood up. "If you talk to Jim, tell him that the mayor needs to speak with him."

"I'll be glad to pass on the message," Lester said. "I'll tell his sergeant to make a note of it."

Mel watched the men leave. It was like Moses parting the Red Sea as they made their way through the precinct. The officers stepped aside, then stood and watched as the men left. There was something about the two that combined power and a sense of something sinister.

"Where is Lavert?" Mel asked.

"He's disappeared," Les said, his face drawn into a frown. "That's virtually an admission of guilt."

"What's your take on the wife?"

"I only spoke to her on the phone. She sounded genuinely upset. Whatever he was into, I don't think she knew anything about it."

Mel nodded. It would be pointless to upset her further, then. "Lester, I need some officers."

"Everyone in this city needs officers. Too bad we don't have the payroll to hire as many as we need. What's this for?"

Mel brought out copies of the photos that had been taken of Lily and the woman in Lily's car. "I need an identification on her." He pointed to the curvaceous blonde behind the wheel.

"Is she a suspect in a murder?" Lester shook his head as he spoke. "Why do you need to identify her?"

Mel knew this was where his normally supportive boss would hit the ceiling. "It's that abandoned baby. The case comes up in court today, about the Johnsons being awarded temporary custody. After the armed attack yesterday, I've been giving this case a lot of thought—"

"This isn't your jurisdiction." Lester's voice was cold steel. "We have ten unsolved homicides from last week. One of them is a woman that the mayor has turned into a poster girl for police incompetence. I want you on that case, not wasting your time trying to find the mama of some doorstep baby.''

''There's more to this case than just an abandoned baby.'' Mel knew he had about ten seconds to make his arguments. ''The Johnsons were attacked. The attacker wanted the baby. Lily Markey is involved in this somehow. My gut tells me—''

''That sounds like a line from some bad television show about cops. Gut doesn't count for much in today's world, Haskin. Evidence is what matters.''

''Gut is the only thing a good police officer has sometimes, and I've learned to trust mine. I've never been wrong. This baby business is deep. It's got ties into our own police department. Maybe even the mayor's office.'' He was pushing it to the extreme, but he had to come up with something big enough to warrant the expenditure of man-hours.

''The mayor's office?''

''There's a tie. Lavert. He may have been acting on his own, but he may not. Can we afford to let it go by without investigating?''

''We can't *afford* an investigation. How many men do you need?''

''Three.'' Mel needed a dozen, but three would work.

''For how long?''

''Just today.'' He needed them for at least a week, but he could make it happen.

''Three men, eight hours. That's the limit. And you'd better bring me something solid and not more of this mumbling about gut.''

Mel grinned. Lester never gave in without grumbling. "I'll bring you something."

"Take Tanner, Chisholm and Barrett."

"Thanks."

"Don't thank me. Just bring me results."

Chapter Ten

Lily awoke to the sound of voices outside the window of her bedroom. Sunlight streamed across her bunk, and she sat up, terrified for a moment. She wasn't certain where she was or who was talking. Gradually, she understood that the gentle movement of her bed was because she was on a boat. The past night came back to her in a rush. She swung her feet over the bunk and hit the floor. She was already dressed.

"Familiar was adamant that we come here," a female voice said. "He was having a conniption this morning."

"He's up to his eyeballs in something," a male voice agreed.

Lily recognized the deep, male voice. Peter Curry, the veterinarian. Also, the owner of the boat. She and Susie were trespassers. She took a breath. There was no help for it. She'd have to simply face up to the truth. But who would believe that a black cat had led them to the boat, given them the key and insisted that they stay there?

Even at the thought of it, Lily knew she sounded

worse than psychotic. She sounded delusional. She didn't have to worry about going to jail for abandoning babies—she was headed for a breaking and entering/trespassing charge in less than two minutes.

Susie was still asleep, and Lily had the added worry that her identity would be revealed. The true implications of that struck Lily with force. If Susie were arrested, Wayman Bishop would have her within his clutches in record time. Wayman had men inside the police department. Damn!

She took a breath and hurried up to the deck. Best to confront the Currys directly. Of course the black cat was nowhere in evidence.

As she climbed the narrow stairs, sunlight touched her face. She saw the Currys, and they were both staring directly at her.

"I can explain, but I don't think you'll believe me," Lily said, walking up on the deck so they could see she was unarmed.

"Familiar brought you here." Eleanor Curry's voice was matter-of-fact.

"You...believe that?" Lily was stunned.

"I know he's been very involved in what's happened with the Johnsons and that baby. I'd have to be blind not to notice that every time something happens involving little David, you're on the scene. What I want to know is—what role are you playing in this, and will the Johnsons be hurt?"

At the sound of footsteps behind her, Lily turned. Susie stood on the stairs, most of her body exposed.

"Lily was helping me," Susie said. "Is David okay?"

Eleanor exchanged a glance with Peter, who'd so far remained silent.

"I don't think we want to hear any more," Peter said, putting his hand on Eleanor's shoulder. "Familiar brought you here, so that must mean he's helping you. Just reassure us that the best interest of that infant is being served by all of this."

"Protecting that child is our sole purpose," Lily said. "I'm sorry the Johnsons have been put in the line of fire. I had no way of knowing such a thing would happen. But if anyone can protect David, they can."

Eleanor nodded. "And the baby will remain with them?" She looked past Lily and directly at Susie.

Lily knew that both Peter and Eleanor had figured out who Susie was. They might not know her name— in fact they obviously didn't want to know—but they knew she was David's birth mother. They were protecting the interests of their friends, the Johnsons.

Susie's voice was filled with emotion as she answered. "A choice was made. David's safety and future happiness is the most important thing."

"Is a legal adoption out of the question?" Peter asked.

"Absolutely!" Lily didn't give Susie a chance to answer. Wayman Bishop would never allow his son to be taken from him. "The father is a...he's abused my friend. He would never legally relinquish his son. We've considered all options. The best for everyone is for little David to remain an abandoned child, without known parents. Trust me. That's absolutely the best plan. For everyone.''

Once again, Peter and Eleanor exchanged looks. "You're welcome to stay on the boat," Peter said, "as long as you want. There's plenty of food in the galley. Help yourself. And call us if we can help you with anything.''

Lily nodded. "Thank you. One day maybe you'll understand this whole mess.''

Eleanor and Peter linked hands. "Maybe, maybe not. Just be careful.'' They turned around and stepped back onto the dock and walked away.

Eleanor turned back. "Stick with Familiar," she said. "He's quite extraordinary. If you listen to him, he can help you.'' She didn't give Lily a chance to respond. She interlocked her fingers with her husband's and they left without another backward glance.

"I thought we were going to jail," Susie said.

"Me, too.'' Lily knew she needed a few moments to digest what had just happened. Four adults had all agreed that a black cat was intelligent enough to govern their behavior.

"What are we going to do?"

Lily heard the sirens headed their way before she could answer. She grabbed Susie and they fled down the stairs. Her first thought was that Peter and Eleanor had gone to the nearest phone and turned them in. But the sirens continued to the next pier, and the two women peeked out a porthole and watched as three units and an ambulance slammed to a halt.

It was only a matter of minutes before Lily knew exactly what was happening. They'd found a body in the Potomac. Judging by the squad cars, the number of men, the bustle of forensic officers, it did not appear to be an accidental drowning.

"There's that detective," Susie said, pointing Mel out as he strode over the pier toward the scene. "He's a handsome man," she added. "Not that I'm a bit interested in men, handsome or otherwise."

Lily couldn't help a slight grin. For just a moment, Susie had sounded like the healthy young woman she should have been, instead of a wife so severely abused she had given up her baby. But it gave Lily hope, hope that Susie would heal and recover her life.

"I wonder who drowned?" Susie asked.

"Might not be a drowning," Lily replied.

"A murder?" Susie waved a hand. "These are expensive boats, an exclusive neighborhood. What are you thinking, a robbery?"

"Or a domestic." Lily spoke before she thought of the consequences. But Susie only frowned and nodded.

"I have to keep reminding myself that domestic abuse can happen at any socio-economic level. I mean, it happened to me. I guess sometimes I pretend so hard that it didn't that I actually forget."

"Forgetting isn't a bad thing," Lily said gently. "Why don't we make some breakfast and then try and decide what we should do?"

"I make the best French toast in the city," Susie said.

Once again Lily felt hope. Susie was coming back to life. "Sounds great. I'll make some coffee."

Lily snapped on the radio to catch the morning broadcast of public radio. There wasn't a television on the boat, and the radio programming contained national news. Her mind was on the drowning victim. And Mel Haskin.

He was everywhere she turned. It was almost as if fate threw him in her path. He was on one side of town investigating a baby and now on the waterfront on an apparent murder. Wherever she went, there he was.

And he *was* a handsome man. She looked out the porthole and saw that he'd left the dock. She could easily visualize him, though. He was tall and well muscled, and smart, too.

Too smart.

Mel was on to her. He wasn't sure what he had, but he knew he had something. And he wasn't going to let it go. Troubled, yet vaguely excited by that thought, Lily put her attention to helping Susie at the stove.

MEL NODDED as he listened to the deputy coroner's initial verdict. Jim Lavert had been shot once in the head, assassination-style, then dumped in the water. He'd been dead before he was immersed.

Mel looked down at the man and felt the slow pull of sorrow that came from any death, even that of a scumbag like Lavert. This man had tried to kill him, and now he was dead. Mel felt no vindication, just the old, tired sorrow that had become part of his job.

''Get me all the facts you can,'' he told Kenny Banks, the coroner.

''Sure thing, Mel. Should have something for you by six.''

''Tonight?'' Mel asked.

Kenny shrugged. ''I got five ahead of you. It isn't exactly my idea of a fun day.''

''Thanks,'' Mel said, knowing Kenny would work as fast as he could.

Mel wasn't surprised that Jim Lavert was dead. One officer didn't fire at another. He'd been into something way over his head. And his employer had judged him as dangerous and expendable. So he'd been removed.

Mel's best lead into the abandoned baby had also been destroyed. So, he had to find a new avenue of clues.

He looked out over the graceful beauty of the boats at the dock and wondered why someone would bring a body here to dump it—right in the lap of the wealthy.

What if the body wasn't brought here? What if the murder had taken place right in this marina?

''I think I'm going to canvass some of the boat owners,'' he said to the other officers who were busy with various aspects of investigating the murder.

''Eyewitnesses?'' one officer asked.

''Ear witnesses,'' Mel said, lifting both eyebrows. ''If we're lucky.''

''Good luck.'' The man turned back to his job.

Mel started with two boats on the dock where the body had been found, but he knew that with the current there was no telling exactly where the body had been dumped.

Many of the boats were empty, and he worked his way over to a houseboat that had caught his eye. It was a beauty, with a huge deck filled with chairs that looked inviting, and what must be a pretty accommodating cabin. Now if one had to be stuck on a boat, that was the kind to be on.

He headed toward it.

"POUR THE COFFEE," Susie said, pulling Lily back from her thoughts.

Lily obliged and realized that the galley had filled with a most delicious odor. Her stomach rumbled in anticipation as she sat at the tiny table while Susie put breakfast in front of her.

"Yum," she said, pouring maple syrup on her French toast.

They'd both just begun to eat when someone knocked on the top of the deck.

"This is the police. We'd like a word with you."

Susie almost choked on her coffee. Lily jumped to her feet, hand out to shush Susie.

"It's probably routine. To find out if we heard anything last night. I'll handle it."

Her heart was pounding, but she had to go and speak with the officer. She hurried up the short stairwell and stepped out onto the deck—beside Mel Haskin.

As their eyes met, she felt her heart turn cold. Mel's face reflected a deep, deep suspicion.

"Detective Haskin," she said, determined to hang on to her cool. "What are you doing out on the river?"

"That's exactly the question I want you to answer," Mel said. His grip on Lily's arm was firm. "I've had enough of this game," he said, anger in his tone. "You keep turning up in the wrong place, Lily. Now you're going to tell me why."

Lily didn't resist him. Instead, she led him to some chairs on the deck. The one thing she couldn't afford was to let him find Susie.

MEL'S INITIAL SHOCK, almost instantly replaced with anger, gave way to a deep suspicion. How was it possible that Lily Markey appeared at every turn of his life? He didn't buy for a second the idea that she was vacationing on a houseboat. She wasn't the type for middle-of-the-week vacations. She was too much like him—always on the job.

He saw a smudge of syrup on her mouth and realized he'd interrupted her breakfast. "You can talk to me while you finish eating," he said, starting to turn back to where he knew the galley must be.

"I'm through." Lily held her ground. "Let's stay up here in the sunshine. So tell me what happened on the next dock. I saw the officers and the ambulance. I figured a murder."

"Is that right?" Mel liked the way she went right to the heart of the matter. She must have seen him at the crime scene, and she wasn't going to pretend she hadn't. "We had a murder, yes."

"Domestic?"

"Doubtful. The man was shot in the temple with a .22."

"Assassination? Gangland murder?" Lily asked, her face registering her surprise. "Here?"

"Maybe. Or the body could have been dumped."

"Here?" she asked again.

Her reaction confirmed everything Mel had initially thought. This marina wasn't a likely place for a murder, nor was it a dumping ground for bodies. But one or the other had happened.

"Yeah, it was one of the mayor's security men," he said casually, "a police officer."

He saw the color drain from her face. She fought to keep her composure and hide the sudden fear in her eyes. Finally she held an expressionless mask on her face.

Mel felt his own emotions fluctuate. The idea that someone had frightened Lily made him angry. Then he was angry at her for getting herself into something dangerous. And then he was coolly curious about why the death of a security man should frighten Lily Markey, star reporter. He felt the odd twitching in his gut and knew he was on the right track. He just had to find the right question.

"What are you really working on, Lily? Have you got something on Mayor Torrell?"

Lily didn't answer immediately. He could see she was trying to determine how much he knew. Good! Mel was excellent at bluffing.

"I'm not working on a story about the mayor in any regard."

"Just his employees," Mel said. He could see that he'd scored a direct hit.

"Why don't you ask me about the murder?" Lily said. "That *is* why you're here, to talk to the people in the boats and see if they saw or heard anything suspicious. Well, I didn't hear a thing. I didn't see a thing. I was sound asleep, I suppose." She rose as if she'd concluded their talk.

"Are you here alone?" Even as Mel asked the question he felt a stab of jealousy. He'd never considered that she might have a man downstairs waiting for her return. He wasn't a boat man, but the idea of spending a night with Lily on board *The Illusion,* as the houseboat was called, was more than enticing.

Lily bit her bottom lip. "Yes," she said. "I came out here for some privacy, a chance to think."

There was something in the way she lowered her gaze that made Mel suspicious. Lily wasn't a very good liar. His gaze drifted toward the stairs and the area of the boat that would house the bedrooms. He stood up and walked that way.

Lily darted around him, blocking his path. "Unless you have a search warrant, you can't go there," she said.

Mel was surprised at her extreme reaction. If she was with a man, it wasn't a federal offense. They were consenting adults. He found a hard pleasure in pushing her buttons.

"If you don't have something, or someone to hide,

what's the problem with me taking a look?'' he asked. Who was it Lily was with? The question was like a thorn in his flesh.

''It's principle, Haskin.'' Lily stood up straight, like a warrior princess. She wasn't backing off an inch, and he felt his estimation of her rise. She was one big pain-in-the-butt, but he liked the way she handled herself. She wasn't the kind of woman who would ever find herself in a place she didn't want to be.

''Principle, or something to hide?'' As much as he admired her, now he wanted to know who she was with. It would be better to confront the facts and get over all of his ridiculous fantasies. That was exactly what he needed, a dose of cold water thrown on his foolish hopes.

''Unless you have a warrant, you'll never know,'' Lily said. She shifted so that her body blocked him.

Mel took a step closer. The average person would automatically back up an inch. Lily didn't. She held her ground and looked up at him.

Mel could see each individual eyelash. They were thick and full, deep black against her ivory skin. And her eyes were an amazing swirl of color. There was the deep green that he knew from her moments of anger, but mixed in were those bits of golden brown and shades of teal. He found himself unable to look away.

When he did finally glance away, it was down to her lips. They were full and generous and just slightly parted. Almost as if they were awaiting a…kiss.

The idea that someone waited down below to kiss

Lily was a spur that Mel could no longer ignore. Way in the back of his brain, a tiny voice told him he was insane, that he was committing professional suicide, that he was acting on an impulse he would regret the rest of his life.

He didn't listen.

He lowered his face slowly to hers, giving her every chance to back away from him. His hands stayed at his sides, and he didn't even lift a finger. But he knew Lily wouldn't back up. She wasn't that kind of woman.

And when his lips settled over hers, he felt a connection so sure and solid that he wasn't even surprised when she kissed him back. Fate had thrown them together for a reason, and as Mel experienced the kiss, he was beginning to believe he might have found out why.

Whatever concerns or objections Lily might have in the future, she had none now. His hands slowly moved to her waist, pulling her into his arms as he held her tightly and deepened the kiss.

For a long time, Mel gave up all rational thought and simply allowed himself the luxury of paradise.

Chapter Eleven

Lily had the strangest sense that she was dreaming. Mel Haskin threatened her very future—and yet the second she knew he was going to kiss her, she lifted her lips and accepted his kiss.

Not only accepted, she responded.

As his arms closed around her, she felt as if she had no other choice. Her body responded to Mel in such a way that her mind was almost disengaged. She wanted only to deepen the kiss, to feel him pressed against her, all solid and strong.

She'd wanted to kiss him for a long time. That much she suddenly knew. And it was a revelation. She hadn't allowed—or admitted—an attraction to a man for a long time. Mel, though, was extremely desirable. He worked on her, big time. In any other circumstances, she might have been tempted to spend the rest of the day exploring all the different sensations his kiss evoked.

But it was concern for Susie that finally made her gather her wits and step back from his strong body.

Her first priority was protecting Susie. And she'd do it no matter what it cost her.

She sighed, looking directly into his eyes, knowing that she had to keep Mel from going below. "There's no one below deck," she said. "Can you trust me on this?"

She could see she had him over a barrel. He could hardly demand a tour now. They'd both crossed a line—one that would be very hard to redraw. Lily took another breath, knowing that it was as ragged-sounding as Mel's. The passion that had been ignited hung between them. All it would take would be one little touch, one whisper. This time, she didn't know if she'd have the strength to force herself out of Mel's arms. For that split second, she'd felt as if nothing had mattered but kissing Mel. It was the most extraordinary feeling—exciting—wonderful, simply exhilarating.

Suddenly Lily knew she'd never been on such dangerous ground.

"Where will you be this evening?" Mel asked, finally getting his breathing back under control.

"At home."

"May I take you to dinner?"

Lily felt a flush creep up her cheeks. Somehow they'd gotten everything backwards. They'd kissed and now he was asking her out on a date. She'd lied to him, and now he was wanting to pay for her dinner. "I think we probably do need to talk," she said. There had to be some way she could explain things to Mel so that he'd back off and let her do what she had to do.

"Yes." Mel stepped back. "You need to tell me the truth, Lily. I don't know what's going on, but I know you're involved. I've got a lot of reasons for not wanting to see you hurt."

She was looking directly into his eyes, and she saw sincerity. She felt lower than a toadstool about lying. "I'll be careful," she promised.

"I'll pick you up at eight, okay? Then we'll talk about abandoned babies and murdered security men."

Where were the million and one excuses that she could roll so easily off her tongue when other men tried to woo her? "Eight will be fine," she said.

Mel looked around the boat one more time. "I'd better get on this case." He stepped away from her, then turned back. "Is this your boat?"

"No. It belongs to a friend." She left it vague. Mel was a smart man. It wouldn't take him two seconds to put the Currys right in line with the Johnsons, and then they'd be back at baby David.

"Must be a very generous friend," he said.

"Yes." She smiled. "See you tonight."

She turned away, afraid that he might ask more probing questions. She had to get Susie off that boat, onto a plane and get her own butt back to the newspaper office. On top of all her worries about Susie's safety, she was going to be in the doghouse at work. Her story wasn't finished—wasn't even close. Her boss was going to pop a gasket.

She met Susie in the hallway, her face still pale from the scare Mel had given her.

"It's okay," Lily said. "I'm going in to the office, and I want you to stay here. I'll figure out a safer place for us and come back as soon as I can."

Susie walked back toward the cabin. "That man, the dead one in the river. He worked for Wayman."

"I know," Lily said, wondering what it must be like to suspect the father of your child of murder.

"Wayman deliberately put him here. He knows where we are. He's been watching us."

Lily grabbed her shoulders. "No, Susie. He doesn't. If he had a clue, he'd be on us like a duck on a june bug. You know that."

Susie turned around, her dark eyes large with fear. "I don't know anything, except that I'm scared."

"I have to go to the office. Will you be okay?"

Susie nodded. "I don't have a choice." Her face crumbled as she sobbed. "Maybe I should get David and go back to him. Maybe he would forgive me and not hurt the baby."

Lily felt the terror snake through her body. She'd heard her sister say the exact same thing. And every time she'd gone back, she'd been beaten a little worse than the last time.

"Promise me you won't go anywhere until I get back," Lily said. "I won't be over an hour. When I come back, we'll find a safe place for you. I promise."

"Okay," Susie agreed, but her voice held no life. Only fear.

"CRAWFISH PIE, jambalaya, filet gumbo, son-of-a-gun gonna have some fun down on the bayou!"

It's a great song, but it doesn't work well on the Potomac. Of course, this is a river, not a bayou. Still there's the wonderful smell of water and seafood and the lifestyle of those who enjoy traveling by water. But this isn't Louisiana. Not by a long shot. Not the right spirit of live and let live. At least, not with Jim Lavert floating around in the water. Well, it isn't polite to be gleeful about death, but I have to say it couldn't have happened to a more deserving guy.

Unfortunately, this bodes poorly for Lily and Susie—if Wayman Bishop catches them. It's been an interesting morning, watching the cops investigate a murder here on the docks. It hasn't been difficult to stay out of sight. No one is looking for a black cat. Right now, though, Lily has something other than babies and bullets on her mind.

So, things are heating up between Miss Pulitzer and the hard-boiled detective. I came along just in time to view the kiss. Wasn't that something? Whenever the two of them are together, the passion in the air is thick enough to cut with a knife. And it's taken them how long to finally act on all that sexy chemistry?

And now I can't stay to congratulate Lily on being brave enough to take a chance on a little love. I've got my work cut out for me with the copper. Lily's lips may have softened him up enough that I can make some headway. This looks like it may be my only chance.

Clotilde is home, asleep. And Preston has hired pri-

vate guards around the house to protect Rose, little David and my lady love. I'm glad to see that. I had a sleepless night last night trying to patrol the area.

I'm about on my last paw today. I need sleep and rich, fatty calories. Hmm, preferably the calories and then the snooze. But I need to talk to Mel more. Somehow, I've got to make him see reason about baby David.

I fully understand where he's coming from. As a kitty who grew up on the hard streets, I think abandonment is one of the worst crimes. But there are extenuating circumstances. The question is, how to make Mel see this?

I'm sure there are books and movies that make this point, but I don't think I can drag a full-grown man into a movie theatre. Not likely. And I'd be willing to bet Mel hasn't had his library card punched in a while.

I suppose what I need to do is go by his place and check it out. Maybe I can find something there that will allow me to start his old thinking train down another track. Good thing I looked up his address where my paws could do the walking. His place is on the way to my humble abode. Ah, the thought of my pillow in the sunny window. Eleanor has taken to her garden like a robin, and I can sleep on the velvet and watch her whenever I open an eye. The April sun is shining. All that lovely red velvet will be warm and soft and just purr-fect for a nap. If I weren't such a dedicated puss, I'd head straight home, dig some leftovers out of the fridge and curl up on my pillow.

There goes Mel. And he's going to have a little black shadow tagging along, whether he knows it or not.

MEL CLIMBED into his car and drove away from the river. He thought of the woman who'd been photographed in the car with Lily. He'd been so jealous at the idea that Lily was with a man that he hadn't even considered that the mystery woman might be sharing the houseboat with Lily. Was that who Lily was hiding? Because she was definitely hiding someone. Or something. She was playing a very dangerous game.

He thought about the fact that Lily had lied to him. He'd told a few stories in his life. Some to spare the feelings of someone else. Some to protect someone. Some because he knew that a lie was the only way to get the truth.

Why had Lily lied to him? The answer to that would determine how much he allowed himself to feel for her. God knew he couldn't stop himself from wanting her. She was one sexy woman, and even the thought of her made him crazy. If he thought about her lips, he'd have to turn around and go back for another kiss.

"You're a fool, Haskin," he said out loud as he cleared the entrance to the marina and headed downtown.

"Meow."

The cat startled Mel, but once he made sure it was Familiar, he realized he'd accepted the cat's uncanny ability to appear in the most unlikely places. "So, you're on the waterfront, too. Next thing I know Preston and Rose Johnson will appear with that baby in a stroller.''

"Me-ow." The cat patted the steering wheel, finally hooking a few claws into Mel's hand. Just enough to get him to turn the wheel.

"If it weren't absolutely insane, I'd think you knew where you were going."

Familiar only dug his claws in a little deeper, demanding a right-hand turn.

Mel obliged. He had plenty to do, but the cat was fascinating. He'd give him a few minutes.

Familiar helped Mel negotiate the streets. When Mel recognized where they were going, he gave the cat a lot of assistance.

"I need to check my messages anyway," Mel said, shrugging at the idea that the cat had taken him home. "But I have to warn you, I'm headed to the office very shortly."

He parked, and the two of them went inside. He watched as Familiar walked through the house, inspecting his modern paintings and the sparse furnishings.

"Not much of a home, is it?" Mel asked. He picked up the phone and punched in his code. He had four new messages.

Lester Bennett was checking on him. Mayor Torrell left an urgent message for Mel to call his office— immediately. There was one hang-up call, and, at last, a call from Officer Chisholm.

"We got some leads on that woman in the photo," Junior Chisholm said in the recorded message. "Call us. We'll stop by your house. I think that might be the wisest thing.''

Mel didn't have to think it over. He punched in Chisholm's number and told the three officers to hustle on to his place. He put on a pot of coffee and watched the feline continue to thoroughly investigate his house as he waited for his officers to arrive.

The cat was fascinated by his small collection of videos. Mel preferred to catch a movie at the theatre when it first came out, but he had acquired a few tapes. While the coffee brewed, he walked over and watched the cat nose through them.

''Nothing too extreme,'' he said. ''No copies of *Wild Kingdom* or *The Lion King*.'' He was amused when Familiar gave him a glare.

''Sorry, cat. I didn't mean to seem impertinent.'' And then he laughed out loud, realizing that he was carrying on a conversation with a feline—who actually seemed to understand what he was saying.

Familiar's black paw patted a movie, sliding it out of the rack.

''You want to watch *Fried Green Tomatoes*?'' Mel opened the movie and slotted it into the VCR. ''You've got about twenty minutes. Then I'm taking you right back to the Johnsons. I don't know how you manage to get all over town, but I'm carting you home. It'll give me an excuse to check on that family.''

''Me-ow!'' Familiar dug the VCR controls out from between the sofa cushions.

''I've been looking for that everywhere.'' Mel

clicked on the television and started the movie playing. To his amazement, Familiar hit the fast forward button and sat back as if he were actually waiting for a particular segment of the movie.

Mel couldn't help himself. He eased down on the sofa to see what the cat would do next. When Familiar patted the control once again, the image on the screen was of a young woman badly beaten. Familiar hit the freeze frame and then leaped from the sofa. In a moment he was back with a picture of the mystery woman in his mouth.

"Meow," he said.

"So you're trying to tell me she's a battered wife." Mel had never been accused of being too sensitive, but he also wasn't dumb as a post. He made the link Familiar was working so hard to point out. "That doesn't excuse abandoning a child. There are laws. There are agencies and places where a woman can go to have her baby and find a proper home for it."

A knock at the door stopped him just as he was building up a head of steam. He hurried to open it and admit the three police officers.

Junior Chisholm had the biggest grin on his face as he stepped through the door. "Have we got news for you," he said. "You'll never guess who the lady in the photograph actually is."

LILY'S EARS were still burning from the harsh words her boss had aimed at her. The worst part was that she knew he was right. She had neglected her job. She'd dropped the ball. Her hands were too full of Susie and baby David.

No matter that she'd gotten a chewing out—she'd made the right decision. And when things settled down and she could actually talk to her boss, she knew she could make him understand. Until then, she'd just have to endure his ire.

She pulled back into the marina, startled to see two more black-and-white police units parked right at the dock where the houseboat was moored.

She got out and sauntered over to the two officers, who were questioning an older woman. The woman was visibly upset.

"She just opened the door, dragged me out of the car and drove off," the woman said. "It was awful."

"Did you get a good look at her?" the officer asked.

"Dark hair and eyes. She was medium height. Just average—except for the look on her face. She was crazy, I tell you. Crazy. She kept yelling that she didn't want to do this, but she had to save her baby."

Lily closed her eyes. She looked toward the houseboat but knew it was empty. Susie was gone. She'd carjacked an elderly woman and now she was on the run.

Without a word to anyone, Lily ran back to her car, jumped in and took off.

"That's her friend!" the old woman yelled. "That's her. I saw them together this morning, out on the deck. Look! She's getting away! Stop her!"

"Hey!" A policeman yelled after her. "Hey, you! Wait up!"

Lily had no intention of heeding his call. She had to get to Susie before Susie tried to get to the baby.

She cut the wheel of the car hard to the right, dodging the policeman, who was actually running after her.

Maneuvering was tight. There was water on two sides of her, and a policeman on the third. Lily had only one direction to go. She pressed the gas pedal to the floor and gripped the wheel tight. With a little bit of maneuvering and a lot of luck, she'd make her escape good.

She headed toward the river, then turned sharply, cutting the wheel so hard the car almost stood on two wheels. It settled back down, hugged the asphalt and shot by the surprised policeman. Lily could see freedom!

Just as she thought she was home free a dark sedan pulled directly into the avenue of her escape. She leaned on the horn, while at the same time stepping on the brakes. Just in the nick of time she brought her car to a halt.

Fury made her jump over the side of the convertible without bothering with the door. She was out and striding toward the black sedan with all intention of telling the driver how close he'd come to meeting his maker. When she was only five feet away, the door opened and Mel Haskin stepped into the morning sunlight.

A sleek black cat leaped out of the car and stood beside Mel, who looked at Lily as if he were considering a lot of possible options—none of them pleasant for her.

Chapter Twelve

Lily sat in the front seat of the car, her lips pressed tightly together. Mel knew exactly how tight they were—he'd studied them closely. He'd researched the way she pressed them more firmly together whenever he asked her a question. How they went completely thin and pale when, after she'd refused to tell him about baby David, he offered her a ride to the precinct house. Or how they'd flushed with anger when he told her that he'd identified the mother of baby David as Susie Bishop. Of course, he'd added how he intended to see that Susie went to jail as an unfit mother.

As he drove toward downtown Washington, he regretted that threat. Truth be told, he regretted his strong-arm tactics with Lily. He could clearly see that if he'd been less forceful, she might have been more forthcoming.

As he cast a sideways glance at her cold profile, he remembered the kiss they'd shared. It was almost as if it were a dream. Nothing in the woman who sat beside him indicated that she might ever have wanted to do anything to him except maybe shoot him or stab him.

"Meow." The black cat sat between them in the front seat. He kept looking from Mel to Lily and back, as if he thought by some miracle they might actually speak to one another.

Familiar nudged Lily with his head, purring loudly.

"Traitor," Lily said bleakly.

"The cat had nothing to do with me finding you," Mel said. "We had the roll of film Jim Lavert took of you and Susie."

That got a reaction from her! She started, let out a gasp and then snapped her mouth shut again.

"Lavert photographed Susie driving your car. He must have followed you from the Johnson house the day of the armed intruder. He had some pretty good shots of you. Susie was a little harder to identify. The blond wig threw us off for a while, but my men finally tracked down her identity." He paused. "If my officers could do it, so could someone else. That was obviously Jim Lavert's assignment—before he was shot in the temple."

His words were having an impact on Lily. She was trembling, and it took all of his restraint not to reach over and soothe her. He couldn't afford to be soft now. Whatever the reasoning behind Susie Bishop's actions, she was going to pay for what she'd done.

"Meow." Familiar nuzzled Lily's elbow, and she finally scooped him into her lap and stroked his sleek coat.

"Familiar and I watched part of a movie this morning," Mel said. If Lily wasn't going to talk, he was at least going to keep the conversation alive. "He seemed to want to make a point to me. Something about spousal abuse. Have any idea what he was getting at?"

Lily's gaze swung to his and held. There was clear assessment in her eyes. Mel regretted that he was driving, because he had to focus on the road.

"I know exactly what the cat was trying to tell you," Lily said, the first words she'd spoken since he'd apprehended her at the marina.

"Do tell," Mel encouraged.

"Sometimes a woman doesn't have a choice, especially when her baby is at risk. You can't imagine someone beating you because the coffee cup wasn't in front of the knife, or because the toilet tissue was hanging the wrong way. If someone took a belt to you, you'd fight back. But not everyone can, Mel. Not everyone has the strength, or the self-confidence."

"Are you trying to tell me that Wayman Bishop beats his wife? The mayor's right-hand man? The person in charge of the latest publicity campaign to make the streets of Washington safe for all women?"

"Susie's been in hiding for nearly two weeks. Wayman doesn't have a clue where she is—or at least, I thought he didn't. There's been no missing-person report filed, has there?"

"Not to my knowledge. But Wayman has the resources to initiate his own private search. The fact that he hasn't filed a missing-person report doesn't mean anything."

"Try checking the emergency-room records at

Lakeland Memorial Hospital. Check and see how many times Susie has been in for broken bones or cuts or burns. Even when she was pregnant.''

"Hospitals are supposed to report spousal abuse. If there had been a report on Wayman Bishop, I would have heard about it.''

"Think, Mel!'' Lily reached across the seat and squeezed his forearm. "Use your brain. Would a woman terrified of her husband say she'd been beaten? No! She fell—she wrecked her car—she walked into a door.''

Lily's touch tingled Mel's skin. She was furious with him—aggravated. It didn't matter. The chemistry between them was so strong that desire spiked through him, and he could see, as she dropped her hand back to the car seat, that she felt it, too.

Mel drove in silence for a few moments, organizing his thoughts. Lily believed passionately in what she was saying. There was no doubt of that. Trouble was, Mel didn't buy her story. Not entirely. Not to the point of thinking it was okay to dump a baby.

"There were avenues open to her. Susie Bishop has a college degree. She was a career woman. She's not some bumpkin from the backside of nowhere. She didn't have to tolerate a husband who beat her. And for that matter, as soon as she knew her baby was in danger, she should have made arrangements. Legal arrangements, to protect herself and the child. That's what a good mother does.''

Lily turned in the seat so that she faced Mel, but he noticed that she was careful not to touch him—not to ignite that wild sensation of want and need. "In a perfect world, yes. I agree with you. But the system doesn't always work. And for someone like Susie, the end result could have been permanent crippling or death, or in her mind something even far worse, an injury to David. Don't you see, Mel, she loved that baby enough to let him go. She cared enough about him to give him the best chance at a good life that she knew how to provide. That's love. That's motherly instinct—doing what's best for the child no matter if it tears your heart out.''

Mel slowed the car and pulled over beside a park. In the distance young children played in the sand and laughed as they swung high in the air on brightly painted swings.

Mel watched the children for a moment before he spoke. ''If you believe so passionately that what she did was right, let's bring her in. Let's put her in protective custody and let a judge decide.''

''And put baby David at risk?'' Lily slowly shook her head. ''I can't do it, Mel. I can't. If Wayman can actually prove that baby is his, he'll take it. And he has the power, the money and the resources to snatch that baby. He'll have Susie ruled as unfit and he'd have total custody of David. Susie's worst nightmare will have come true.''

Mel knew that what he was about to say would be the end of whatever feelings Lily might have for him. ''You assume that baby David will be left with the Johnsons.'' He cast a quick look at her and saw she followed him perfectly. ''As a law officer, I have to return the baby to his natural father.''

He expected an outburst, anger or pleading—something. Lily simply turned around to look out the front windshield and said nothing else.

"Lily, I have to do it."

She didn't answer. Her profile was still, and with her pale, fine skin she looked as if she'd been carved in alabaster. Her beautiful auburn hair ruffled gently in a breeze that came through the open car window.

"In a perfect world, I could ignore my duty," he said, this time more gently.

"Once he has that baby, he'll hunt Susie down like a rabid dog and kill her. Her body will disappear and no one will ever know."

Mel watched Lily as she spoke. She was perfectly composed. It gave him hope that she might be reasonable.

"The way I see it, Susie's best chance is to turn herself in. That way she's on record as the baby's mother. We'll protect her until the custody issue is settled by a court. Surely you can't believe that a judge would give custody of the baby to a violent man?"

"Surely not." There was mocking in Lily's voice. "Nothing like that would ever happen in Washington, D.C."

"It's the best I can offer you," Mel said. He wanted to touch her, to gently turn her face so that she would look at him.

Lily was about to respond when the radio in the car squawked into life. "Car 22, there's been a kidnapping at 1212 Mulberry Lane. An infant has been taken by a woman driving a black Taurus, 1998 model. Do you copy?"

"Damn!" Mel and Lily spoke in unison.

Mel started the car and squealed out into the street, forcing several cars out of the way. They both knew what had happened—Susie had taken baby David from the Johnson home. She was on the run with her baby!

"Can everyone on the police force hear that call?" Lily asked.

Mel nodded, too intent on his driving to answer.

Lily took a deep breath. "Then I'll help you get her. Wayman has access to police calls. He'll know she has the baby, and he'll try to get her now. She and the baby are in terrible danger. If Wayman gets her first, he'll have David and he won't hesitate to really hurt Susie."

"Do you have any ideas how to get in touch with her?" Mel asked as he drove.

"I know where she'll go."

"Where?" Mel was shocked at her sudden cooperation.

"There's a warehouse. Down on 18th Street. That's where we're supposed to meet if anything goes wrong. She'll go there and wait for me to help her get out of the city with the baby."

"Why are you helping me?" Mel asked.

"Because Wayman has men at all levels in the police department. Like I said, Susie won't live past noon if one of them spots her. We're her only chance."

"Even if she may go to jail for abandoning her baby?" Mel wanted to make it perfectly clear that although he was trying to sympathize with Susie's plight, his first priority was the baby.

"Jail is better than a coffin," Lily said bleakly.

"Right. Give me the directions."

SITTING IN LILY'S lap is one of the wonders of the world. She's soft and tender and...determined. Now we have to focus on helping Susie. I'm not so certain that official custody is the best step, but now that Susie's added abduction to her list of crimes, she's in for a rocky legal road.

I'm just glad that Mel's a good driver. The speed we're going is making even me nervous. I think the best thing to do is burrow into Lily's lap and pray that if we come to a sudden halt, she remembers to hang on to me.

We're headed down into an industrial section. There's the warehouse, and Mel is whipping the car into a parking space. Well, sort of. I guess with an official vehicle we can just leave it sticking out in the street.

Here we go. As they used to say on Miami Vice, *it's show time.*

MEL SLIPPED his gun out of the shoulder holster. "Stay in the car," he told Lily.

"I have to go in with you. Susie won't come out unless she knows I'm here."

Mel started to object, then decided not to. "Lily, this could be very dangerous."

"More so for Susie than anyone else." Lily opened the door and stepped into the street. She looked at the black cat. "Familiar should stay in the car."

"Right. Stay put, cat." Mel motioned Lily to get

behind him as he led the way into the darkened interior of the warehouse. "Where will she be?"

"Over there." Lily pointed to the back where a small office door hung open.

"Call her out."

"It would be better if we went to her," Lily said. She started forward.

Mel grabbed her shoulder. "Stay behind me," he ordered tersely.

"Whatever you say." Lily fell in behind him.

Mel could feel her. He was acutely aware of her, even as he focused all of his attention on the interior of the warehouse. It was a perfect place for disaster. There were boxes and crates—plenty of hiding places for the enemy. But if Susie was there, he intended to find her and take her to the safety of the precinct house. Her and the baby.

Together Mel and Lily moved forward. Careful inch by inch they made their way to the open office door.

"Wait here," Mel said. It was so quiet in the warehouse. Susie and the baby must be terrified.

"Okay," Lily agreed. "But let me call out to her."

Mel glanced all around. They seemed to be alone. "Okay."

"Susie, it's me," Lily said. "We're coming to help you. Mel's coming in. Don't panic. We're going to make it all work out."

Mel gave her one quick look. "Thanks," he said. "I will do the best for her I can."

Lily nodded, her gaze falling to the floor. "We're both caught in a situation, Mel. I understand that."

He took a deep breath and darted forward across the

open space, rolling. He came up on his feet at the door of the office. In one fluid motion he burst through the door and into the dark room.

He was still trying to judge the interior of the space when he heard the office door slam behind him, shutting out even the small amount of light. There was the sound of a bolt sliding home.

"I'm sorry, Mel," Lily said. "You didn't leave me a choice. As soon as Susie and the baby are safely on a plane, I'll come and let you go."

"Lily! Lily, don't do this! You're going to be in serious trouble." He tried to contain his anger. She'd tricked him. And he'd fallen for it like a rookie. "Lily, let me out and we'll forget this ever happened."

"I can't, Mel."

He could hear regret in her voice, and it only added fuel to his anger. "Lily, think about what you're doing."

He waited for her to reply, but there was only silence. He knew that she was gone.

LILY HURRIED back outside, taking care to close the warehouse door. It was a good thing she knew the owner of the building. In fact, she'd been looking at it as a possible investment. Though it was crammed with boxes and crates, it wasn't being used. Mel would be safe there until she could return and release him. Then she'd face whatever consequences came of her actions.

And there would be some. Mel would nail her to the wall. She didn't doubt it for an instant.

She got in the car, surprised that the black cat had

disappeared. She could only hope that Familiar was as good at getting home from the warehouse district as he was from other areas of town, because she didn't have time to hunt for him. She had to find Susie and the baby—before Wayman did.

Where had Susie gone? Where was there left for her to hide? None of her former friends would help her. She wouldn't go to any of the shelters for abused women. Where?

She racked her brain trying to think. There weren't many options open to a woman who was hiding from a powerful man. And Susie had been identified by the police. She was the quarry for every hunter in town. A shelter for battered women was out of the question. Wayman would have his men watching like hawks.

Susie had no family. No relatives who might risk themselves in an attempt to aid her. Where would she go?

Lily headed toward the Johnsons'. Susie wouldn't be there, but it was a place to start. As she got closer and closer to the wealthy residential area, she had a sudden thought. Once before, they'd driven past a small, private park. Susie had made the comment that when she'd first gotten pregnant with David, she'd daydreamed about playing in the park with her child, like all the other mothers. She'd fantasized about what it would be like to love her child and anticipate returning home to a loving husband.

It wasn't much of a chance, but it was the only place Lily could think to begin. She drove toward Amberly Park and pulled up beneath a blossoming dogwood tree.

The sound of children's laughter filtered into the car on a soft breeze. She had a flash of sitting at the park with Mel as she tried to make him understand about Susie. Why was he such a hardheaded man? Why couldn't he recognize that not everyone was as strong as he was? She realized her fists were clenched on the steering wheel, and her eyes had filled with tears.

Angrily she wiped them away. Mel had forced her to do what she did. His own stubbornness had made her lock him in the warehouse. Of course, a jury wouldn't see it that way when she was tried for... what? Abducting a police officer? Kidnapping? How bad was it going to be?

"Plenty bad," she said out loud as she opened the car door and got out.

In the distance happy children laughed and ran. They were mostly toddlers, almost all with an adult hovering over them. Lily watched them for a moment. Yes, if Susie had a chance at this life, then whatever the cost, it would be worth it.

She saw a tall, slender woman calling to a toddler who was stuck at the top of a slide. The little boy was afraid to go down, and his mother gently encouraged him, her arms open wide to catch him.

For one blinding moment, Lily thought she recognized the woman. She looked exactly like Lily's sister, Babs. But Babs didn't have a toddler. And she never would.

In a fit of rage, Bobby Reynolds had made sure of that. He'd used his fists to destroy the baby that Babs carried, and the resulting damage had been so severe that Lily's sister would never be able to carry a child.

"Never again," Lily said softly to herself. She turned and began the search for Susie. She saw her almost instantly, huddled on a park bench with an infant in her arms.

For a long moment Lily simply watched her. Susie was totally absorbed in her child, oblivious to the fact that she could be in danger.

"Oh, Susie," Lily whispered as she started forward. "What am I going to do with you now?"

She walked up to her and put a hand on Susie's shoulder. The young woman jumped and startled the baby so much that little David began to cry.

"Hush, now," Susie said. "You're with your mom. Everything's okay." She cradled the baby to her chest and looked up at Lily. "I'm sorry. I just…"

"We'll think of something," Lily said, urging her to stand. "But we can't stay here. Not out in the open. Everyone is looking for you, Susie. The police have identified you."

"Wayman?"

"I'm sure he knows," Lily said.

"He's going to kill both of us," Susie said, her face going gray. "He'll kill us without batting an eye."

Chapter Thirteen

Mel, oh Mel. When will you learn? You walked into that like a giant rat racing after a hunk of melted brie. I wondered why Miss Pulitzer was suddenly being so cooperative. Now I know. She had no intention of leading Mel to Susie. Far from it. She's got our erstwhile detective locked up as tight as the gold at Ft. Knox.

I have to hand it to Lily. That was some caper. But the price for success is going to be very, very steep. I can hear ol' Mel in there boiling! Actually, I think there's steam coming off the walls. He is hot!

You know, humanoids are the most irrational species on the planet. I admit, Mel wasn't listening closely to what Lily said. He heard her, but he didn't listen. So she took action.

But now he'll never listen. And he's got that Barney Fife attitude that the guilty are going to pay. He needs a little more of Andy's wisdom sprinkled into his thought processes. But it's a little late for that now. Lily has just jumped to the top of his guilty list. In his opinion, she's B-A-D!

Well, I have a couple of choices. I can help Mel get out of this, or I can figure out a ride back to check on my Clotilde. She's been there alone all day, and what with baby David being abducted—even though I know it was by Susie, and I'm sure Clotilde recognized her—Rose and Preston are going to be distraught. My darling will have her hands full, but she's a capable puss.

Ah, my Clotilde. That's where my heart lies. My loyalty rests, I suppose, with Mel. While he's stubborn, ornery, willful, hard-of-hearing, aggressive and misguided, he's also a lot like me. The women call it testosterone poisoning. Not necessarily a physical condition, but a mental state. Mel suffers from an advanced case of it, I fear.

I guess I'd better help him escape. Not because he needs to be free, but because I have a really bad feeling that Lily and Susie are going to need him, and very soon.

This Wayman Bishop character, though I haven't had the pleasure, sounds like a man who will stop at nothing. If he kills Susie, he'll have to kill Lily first. Therefore, it would be in the best interest of the two women, and baby David, if Mel were around to play Supercop. A little more Marshal Dillon is the way I'd describe it.

Let me see. Maybe I can get him to think a few minutes about why he's in the mess he's in. See, I know bipeds are quick to act and slow to think. But I believe they can be taught. It's a slow and tedious process for someone like me, but then, they are the lower species, and we should be kind to them. Really. It's a sign of superior intelligence to show kindness to a creature further down the food chain.

It can also be a mistake—I know. Survival of the fittest doesn't always mean the smartest, or the best. It means the strongest and the most adaptable. There you have it. Cockroaches and bipeds, the two most adaptable species on the planet.

Okay, Mel, now that I have you categorized, I'd better figure out a way to open the door for you. But first, what about a little promise to listen to me and me only. Hey, that's a great idea—a biped with his strength powered by my brain! I wonder where Dr. Frankenstein is when I need him.

MEL HEARD SOMETHING outside the door of the office. It sounded like scratching. He pushed the idea of a big rat out of his mind. Listening, he heard it again, and, though he was hoarse from calling, he yelled again. ''Hey! Somebody, open the door!''

He knew it was a fifty-fifty chance that the someone who came to his rescue would be a friendly type. But he'd cross that bridge when he came to it. And as soon as he got over it, he'd find Lily and wring her neck.

Then he'd sign up at a special school for the completely stupid and gullible. Surely there was a place he could get special training. As mad as he was at Lily, he was furious with himself for falling for her stunt.

''Hey! Open the door!'' He called out again when he heard a scuffling noise outside the locked door.

To his surprise, he heard something sliding along the floor at the bottom of the door. He bent down and picked up a gritty piece of paper. He struck the cigarette lighter he carried in his pocket, revealing a yellowed religious pamphlet.

"Forgiveness is the key to heaven," he read out loud. He tossed the paper down. "I'll show you forgiveness. Whoever you are, if you don't open this door, I promise that I'll make your life a living misery when I *do* get out."

"Me-ow."

"Familiar? Is that you?" He couldn't believe it was actually the cat. Somehow, Familiar had managed to stay behind.

"Get some help," he said. "You can do it. You're the smartest cat in the world." He'd been talking to the cat for several days, what did it matter if he added a little flattery?

There was the sound of something rustling on the floor again and Mel struck the lighter. Another yellowed pamphlet shot under the door bearing the same message.

"Familiar?" He wondered if the cat had lost his mind.

"Me-ow?"

There was a distinct question in the cat's tone. Suddenly he understood. The implication of it made him stiffen his spine. "You want me to forgive Lily?" It was an outrageous demand.

"Meow."

The cat's reply was so soft and sweet that Mel wondered if the little calico had also happened upon the scene. Clotilde was her name. Yes, she was sweet. Not at all like Familiar. The black cat was blackmailing him, for Mel knew the door would never open unless he agreed to Familiar's terms. Forgiveness for Lily.

"I can't," he said.

His reply was met with silence. Mel leaned against the wall. He'd just wait until someone missed him and figured out where he was. But why would anyone even think to look in an old warehouse? He was certain Lily had taken his car. So, until someone caught her and made her talk, he was going to be stuck in a dark room with little air.

"Familiar?" Maybe the cat was still out there.

His answer was another shuffle of paper under the door. He didn't even have to look at it to know what it was.

"I thought you were on my side," he said.

There was only silence.

"Okay, I'm thinking it over. Just don't leave, okay?"

"Meow."

The cat was waiting, but there was an impatience in his tone. Mel sighed. He could sit in the dark for the next five years and he still wouldn't feel any more like forgiving Lily. But he wasn't going to get out until he did. He had a thought.

"What about if I don't forgive her, but I don't prosecute her?"

"Me-ow!"

He nodded. At last they had an agreement. "So how are you going to get me out?"

"Meow," Familiar assured him. "Meow."

Mel had nothing to do but wait. In less than ten minutes he heard the excited voices of several men. The voices drew closer and closer to the door.

"Hey, I'm in here," he said.

"Well, I'll be," one man said. "Where'd that cat go?"

The door opened and Mel blinked at the sudden daylight that hit his eyes—and three burly men who held sticks of wood. "Hey, thanks," he said.

"Who are you?" one of the men asked warily.

"Police Detective Mel Haskin." He flipped his badge. "A...subject locked me in here. I thought I was going to spend the rest of the week there." He looked around for Familiar. "How did you find me?"

"We were chasing this black cat that was foaming at the mouth. Rabies, more than likely." The men looked around. "He came in here. We'd better call animal control."

Mel nodded his head. "Yeah, you'd better. But thanks for letting me out." He hid his grin as he watched the men hustle out of the building, still looking for the rabid cat. As soon as they were gone, Familiar came out from behind a crate. He daintily wiped his mouth with one paw.

"You drive a hard bargain," Mel said. He'd given up at being ashamed of talking to the cat.

Familiar's golden eyes only blinked. Then he ran out into the street, leaving Mel to follow.

LILY REALIZED that she couldn't drive around town for the rest of the day. They'd narrowly avoided being spotted by policemen twice. The lock on the warehouse door was sturdy, but she didn't underestimate Mel. She'd been gone longer than she'd expected. It was possible he'd figured a way out. And when he did get out of the warehouse and reported his car stolen, she and Susie were going to have an even rougher time of avoiding apprehension.

At the idea of Mel in the locked office, she had more than a little twinge of regret. He would never forgive her. Never. The memory of his touch whispered over her skin and the sense of loss was like a physical blow. The next time Mel touched her, it would be to apply handcuffs. He would never kiss her again.

Of course the kiss had been a mistake. Mel would only think now that she'd kissed him as part of some kind of act so that later she could dupe him into the warehouse.

Nothing was further from the truth, though. Lily knew, but she also knew that Mel would never believe her now. He would never believe that the rush of emotion she'd felt in his arms had shaken her entire world.

Lily had always enjoyed men and dating and the routines of courtship and friendship—until Babs. When she'd watched her sister being beaten repeatedly, and continuing to return to her husband for another dose of violence and cruelty, it had done something to Lily. She'd convinced herself that her life was better off without the danger that a man brought with him. Because the truth was, no one believed Babs. None of Bobby's fellow police officers would lift a finger. Not even after Babs lost her baby.

The idea that a woman had no recourse had angered Lily, then frightened her. It was almost as if she'd suffered more harshly from Babs's beatings than her sister had.

Mel would never be able to understand that. In his book, Lily was a lawbreaker. That was the big problem. Mel lived in a black-and-white world, and Lily's was gradations of gray. Two people with such different philosophies would never be able to work out any kind of understanding.

But his kiss had opened a door that Lily had thought was closed tight. Mel had made her remember her sensual side. He'd reminded her that though she was extremely busy and very self-sufficient, she was also lonely. She enjoyed kissing a man. She missed the physical contact. And she suspected that Mel was the only man who could bring that part of her back to life.

And she'd lost him.

Her thoughts were so distressing that she glanced over at Susie. She and the baby were asleep, slanted against the car door. Well, it was a good thing they were getting some rest, because Lily didn't have any ideas about where to go next.

Susie roused slightly, and with her least movement, the baby began to cry.

"We need formula," Susie said, waking fully. "Maybe I could breast-feed him."

"No! We'll stop at a grocery store up here. I'll run

in and get formula.'' Lily knew the bond between Susie and David was already too strong.

It wasn't the best part of town, but Lily knew that no place was really safe for them. She pulled into the parking lot of a rundown Lottafood and hurried inside. She picked up diapers and formula, the basic baby items she knew Susie and David would need. Then what? She pushed that question aside as she paid the cashier and walked out of the store.

At first she thought she was dreaming. Mel's car was making a sharp turn in the parking lot. There was one wild cry from Susie in the passenger side, and Lily caught a fleeting glimpse of a big man at the wheel of the car. One of Wayman's goons, no doubt.

She dropped her purchases to the asphalt and ran after the car. ''Stop! Stop!'' She yelled at the taillights that were speeding away. The car sped into the street, narrowly missing an oncoming vehicle. Then it was gone.

For a long moment, Lily stood in the parking lot. Thoughts tumbled through her head, and all of them spelled disaster for Susie.

The bottom line was that Wayman had somehow tracked his wife. And now he had Susie and baby David.

MEL LEFT the Johnson home with a sinking feeling. There was no doubt that Susie Bishop had abducted her own child. To his amazement, neither Rose nor Preston Johnson were willing to press charges. Their sympathy seemed to be with Susie.

As he took the keys to a police car from one of the officers, he saw that both Familiar and Clotilde were following him.

"Not this time. Go home and stay there," he told them. The one thing he didn't need was two interfering, blackmailing cats. He intended to track Lily and Susie down and bring them both to justice. He'd promised Familiar that he wouldn't press charges against Lily for locking him in the warehouse, but he still had her on aiding in the abandonment of a helpless child. That would be plenty.

To his relief the sidewalk was empty as he unlocked the car and got in. He had to travel light and fast. He was looking for the two women and the baby, but so was Wayman Bishop.

Mel felt his stomach knot, and he realized then that he believed Bishop might kill Lily and Susie. It was a big assumption, but in his gut he knew he was right.

What must it feel like to think that the man you were married to was capable of killing you and getting away with it?

He pushed that thought away. Nothing justified what Susie had done. Nothing.

But he didn't want to see her hurt.

He drove through the neighborhood and headed to Lily's apartment. It was a long shot, but there might be some clue there as to where the three of them had gone.

He spotted the black Taurus sedan as soon as he turned the corner. It was the car Susie had stolen. He didn't have to run the plates to confirm it. Parking behind it, he got out and checked the interior. A tiny baby bootie lay on the floorboard. The sight of it made him sad. He started to run the plates, then decided against it. Lily had said that Wayman Bishop had men at all levels in the police department. Jim Lavert had certainly been on Wayman's payroll. He couldn't risk giving any details of his search for Susie and Lily over the air. He was on his own.

After ten minutes he'd crisscrossed the park and knew that neither Lily nor Susie was there. But they had been. A couple of women remembered them, huddled on a bench and acting strangely. The baby had been with them.

Mel had just gotten back in the patrol car when the radio barked to life.

"Detective Haskin?" the dispatcher said.

"Yes."

"We've got a private message for you."

"Okay."

"We've been given instructions not to broadcast it. You're supposed to come in to the precinct and pick it up." The dispatcher sounded a little unsure.

"I don't have time—"

"The woman said it was urgent. She said she owed you an apology, and she needed your help."

Lily! His pulse jumped at the thought, but he quickly regained control of his emotions. She was the kind of woman who would manipulate him to her own advantage given the tiniest opportunity.

"I'm working on something. I'll be there when I can."

"She said it was urgent. She said that innocence, once lost, can never be regained." The dispatcher lowered her voice. "She's that newspaper reporter. I recognized her, and she's really upset."

Mel felt a strong urge to rush to the precinct and see what had happened to Lily. He forced himself to remain perfectly calm.

"I'll be there when I can," he said.

"Well, I'll tell her that," the dispatcher said a little crossly. "Just hurry, okay? She's about to have a conniption fit, and she said no one could help her but you."

Mel drove fast toward the precinct. What the dispatcher hadn't said, but what was very clear, was that Lily had to be desperate to ask for his help. Something had gone terribly wrong.

THE MINUTE MEL walked in the door, Lily stood. She almost ran across the waiting room to him.

"I know you're mad," she said in a whisper, before he had a chance to say anything. "I don't care what you do to me. Wayman has Susie and the baby. I don't know where they are and I don't know what he'll do to her."

In her concern for Susie, Lily had no regard for herself. Mel could think her a fool, an idiot and a criminal, she didn't care—as long as he helped her save Susie. When Mel took her arm and led her out of the building and onto the sidewalk, she followed him docilely. She wanted a chance to talk to him privately.

"How do you know Bishop has her?"

"She was abducted from a grocery store parking lot. I went inside and Susie waited outside with the baby. When I went out, a man was in the car and driving away. Susie was screaming. Who else would take her?" Lily countered. "You don't have her. If she'd been arrested, someone would have brought her in by now, right?"

Mel ignored her question and countered with one of his own. "What if she left on her own? What if it was all pre-arranged?"

Lily shook her head. "Why? I was only helping her. At least with me she had someone to fall back on. She would never have left me. Never."

"If Wayman has her, what makes you think he'll harm her?"

"He wants the baby. His son. Susie has defied him. He'll never tolerate it. And the plain truth is that he can kill her and get away with it. It's the expedient thing to do."

Mel shook his head. "Lily, if every man hit a woman who defied him, all women would be battered. In fact, you'd be in serious trouble right this minute."

The truth struck Lily with the sureness of a thunderbolt. The reason Mel didn't understand Susie's plight was because he wasn't that kind of man. If he were an abuser, he'd be thinking of a way to hurt her now. Instead, he'd come to help her.

"Mel," she said. Her fingers sought his hand and held on to it. "Please, just listen to me. Wayman has Susie. I know he has. If we don't find her soon, she'll disappear forever. I know this is hard for you to understand because…'' she squeezed his hand tightly ''…because you would never hit a woman or hurt her.'' Her grip tightened and she knew she was hanging on to him, hanging on to the truth she'd just discovered and didn't want to lose.

She saw something in his eyes, something hot that fought against the coldness that he tried to project. She knew then that she had one chance to reach him before he slipped back behind his professional training and his rigid sense of right and wrong.

She lifted her lips to his and kissed him. It took several seconds, but then he responded, kissing her back. For one moment of pure bliss, Lily gave herself to the luxury of the kiss. She let Mel's mouth devour her, and then she gently pulled back from him.

''I have to tell you the truth, Mel. I've never wanted a man like I want you. Never. I know that I may have ruined it, and that will be the price I pay. But don't let Susie die because of me.''

Chapter Fourteen

Mel found himself caught in the pure greenness of Lily's eyes. She took his breath away—with her beauty and with her courage.

She was in more trouble than she'd ever get out of, and yet her concern was for Susie. But for all of her stubbornness—which Mel was more than familiar with—there was also something new. Something had happened to Lily. There was a softness about her that he'd never seen before. It was almost as if she'd finally come to some conclusion that allowed her to drop her guard.

He was about to reach for her again when the blast of a horn penetrated his consciousness and he turned to see a black cat seated behind the steering wheel of a patrol car.

"Familiar," he and Lily said in unison. As soon as they spoke, the more petite little calico's head popped up in the front seat. The horn sounded again, this time longer than before. At the conclusion, Familiar gave it two sharp toots.

"We have to get moving," Lily said. "Familiar

knows that time is the enemy. If we don't get there…''
She was already walking toward the car.

''Where is Susie?'' Mel asked.

''I don't know. She has your car. Or I should say, she was in your car when she disappeared. We can figure out where she is and help her, can't we, Mel?''

Mel opened the passenger door and seated Lily. The two cats huddled in the middle of the front seat. He walked around and got in, slamming the door. ''We can try. If Wayman Bishop does have her, where would he take her?'' he asked.

Lily's fingers drummed on the dash as she thought. ''Not to their home. Probably not to their cabin in the mountains. It would be somewhere that wouldn't be attached to him. Somewhere—where was Jim Lavert killed?''

Mel didn't respond, he picked up the radio and called the coroner's office. In a few moments, he had his answer.

''Forensic evidence indicates Lavert was killed somewhere near the marina.''

Lily's eyes widened. ''Susie said something about when they were first married, they sometimes borrowed a boat for a weekend. The implication was that it was a very nice boat.''

At the look of hope in her eyes, Mel wanted to slam his fist into something. ''Lily, there must be ten thousand boats in that area.''

He saw the hope fade from her eyes. When she spoke her voice was desolate. ''He has her right this minute and there's no telling what he might do to her."

"Meow!" Familiar patted the radio in the car. Beside him Clotilde gave an approving purr.

"What are you trying to tell me?" Lily asked.

Mel looked over at her and caught the half-embarrassed look on her face. "Forget it, Lily. I talk to him, too."

Familiar batted the radio again, this time more aggressively.

"He wants something to do with calling," Lily said. "It has to do with the radio, someone we could call or did call. Is it the coroner?" Lily asked.

Familiar blinked once, a negative.

"Let's see. We called about Lavert..."

"Meow!" Familiar and Clotilde chorused.

Mel nodded slowly. "Not a bad idea. Jim Lavert is the only solid lead we have. We know he's connected, and if we can find someone who will provide us a clue... We should talk to Lavert's widow and see if she knows anything about where he was murdered. There might be something there." He reached over the cats and touched Lily's shoulder. "It's a long shot. Don't get your hopes up." He started the car and pulled into traffic.

"Hope is all I've got left right now," Lily said.

Mel swallowed. His anger at her was gone, like some kind of magical evaporating anger. He'd never experienced this acceptance of another person's actions. Especially not when they'd been directed at making him a prisoner in a warehouse. Still, Lily was gaining nothing by her involvement. Not a single thing. Although the road to hell was often paved with good intentions, he didn't doubt that her intentions were actually good.

"Why are you doing this?" he asked as he dodged the late-afternoon traffic. Although the spring days were lengthening, it would soon be dark. He felt as if he'd been up for at least a week. What with his erotic fantasies about Lily and chasing around after her in real life, the newspaper reporter was taking a heavy toll on his sleep.

"Why am I helping Susie?" Lily gave a half laugh and slowly shook her head. "I never thought it would turn out to be like this. Honestly. I guess I was naive when I started trying to help her. I thought it would be a simple matter of getting her on a plane and into a new life. But then there was the whole issue of the baby. She couldn't fly until he was born. After that…I realized she had no one else. So I couldn't stop."

Mel knew he was on delicate ground. He didn't understand Lily, but he was beginning to trust her reasoning.

"What did you think you would accomplish?" he asked.

He could tell she was weighing his question, wondering if he was trying to elicit information or if he actually wanted to know.

She took a breath. "I hoped to find a good home for the baby, and for Susie to escape and start a new life."

"She couldn't have a new life *with* her child?" Mel asked gently.

"It might have been possible to get her out of the country alone, but you can bet Wayman had every airport under surveillance. With a child, she'd never have been able to board a plane. There wouldn't have been a disguise good enough."

Mel absorbed what she said. "How could she leave her baby?" he finally asked.

"Because she loved him so, and because she wasn't certain she could provide for him properly. Mel, she was going to a new life, a place where she knew no one. She left without a penny. She knew she was going to have to work and put the baby in child care. We knew the Johnsons wanted a child, and we both knew what wonderful parents they would be. It might not be the decision you would make, but then you aren't Susie, and you can never understand, until you've been there."

"I am trying," he said softly, surprised that he was. He turned the car into a driveway and turned off the ignition. Reaching across the seat, he took Lily's hand. "I really am trying."

"I know." She squeezed his fingers.

Mel didn't bother to attempt to keep the cats in the car. They scampered across the lawn and disappeared. He simply took Lily's elbow and guided her to the door. "Let's hope we can learn something useful here."

He rang the bell and a petite blonde opened it. She looked at him, then at Lily. Mel showed his badge and explained that he needed to talk with her about her husband.

Margie Lavert showed them into the den and took a seat across from Lily. Mel took another wing chair. As he settled in he saw the two cats peering in an open window.

"Have you found the person who killed Jim?" she asked, brushing away her tears.

"We're looking. Maybe you can help."

She shook her head. "He never told me anything. He said it was best that I didn't worry. He was gone day and night, and it just got to the point that I didn't expect him to be here. But I always thought he'd come back."

"Mrs. Lavert, do you recall your husband ever mentioning a boat or a place on the water?"

"Not anything we owned," she answered quickly. "That kind of stuff was always in the future, when we retired. Once upon a time, we might have talked about boats and cruises and vacations, but not in the last five years." She hesitated. "Mayor Torrell has a boat he loans the men sometimes."

Mel slipped a notebook out of his pocket and took down the address. "What about Wayman Bishop?"

"No, he never had one to my knowledge. But he and his wife used to borrow the mayor's. It's a nice boat. An old one. We went to some parties there several years ago. The mayor might have sold it. I just don't know."

"And it was moored where?"

"Henderson Marina. Sort of a private place. I

haven't thought of that boat in a while." She brushed away more tears. "Jim said when we retired we were going to buy a sailboat and travel. He always had big plans, but that was his way."

Mel stood. "I'm sorry for your loss, Mrs. Lavert. We'll be in touch."

He got Lily out the door as fast as he could without behaving suspiciously. They both jumped in the car, relieved to see the cats were waiting on the front seat.

"Henderson Marina," Mel said, feeling the twist of his gut that told him he was hot on the trail.

"Where is it?" Lily asked.

"About two miles upriver from where you were. It's very exclusive. Very private." He didn't add, very isolated.

He drove toward the river as fast as he could. With his free hand he took a gun from a holster at his ankle and handed it to Lily. "Take this, just in case. It's my backup."

She took it with reluctance. "I doubt I could hit anyone."

"I hope it doesn't come to that, but I don't want you unarmed. If Wayman Bishop is here with Susie…" He didn't finish. He didn't have to. Lily was smart enough to know that a desperate man was a dangerous one.

"Hurry, Mel," Lily said. Night had begun to fall. It would be full dark before they made it to the river.

Mel reached for the radio, then put it back. "Let's just check it out. If there's anything there, we'll radio in."

Lily didn't say anything. She held the gun by her leg and stared out the window.

Mel made it to the marina in record time. As he headed down a smooth, freshly graveled road he turned off his headlights. The moon was bright enough to light the way, and he didn't want to lose the only advantage he had—surprise.

As the car coasted to a stop he stared at the scene in front of him. He'd seen Henderson Marina on maps before, but he wasn't prepared for the beauty of the place, or the sense that there wasn't another living human for miles around. Wealth had bought Mayor Torrell a huge chunk of privacy. The inlet was on a long narrow channel at least a mile off the river.

At the end of a long pier a beautiful old wooden-hulled boat shifted gently on the current. Except for a light in midship, the boat was dark.

Mel signaled Lily to follow him to a clump of shrubs near the shoreline. He crouched beside her and was relieved to discover that Familiar and Clotilde had joined them. The cats would take care of Lily.

"What are we going to do?" Lily asked in a whisper.

Her lips were beside his ear, and though the situation was dire, Mel wanted to kiss her, to hold her. And much more.

"You're going to wait here and I'm going to try and sneak on board. If I can check things out, we'll have a better chance. If something goes wrong, you can go to the car and radio for a backup. I'd call now, but I can't be certain who's monitoring the frequency.'' He didn't want to mention that a rush of police officers at a hostage situation might also escalate the danger. It would be better for everyone if he could resolve this himself.

Lily reached into the pocket of her jacket and brought out a cell phone. ''Handy tool,'' she said, passing it to him.

Mel took it and quickly dialed the precinct. His eyes met hers and he handed it back. ''The batteries are dead.''

''Damn!'' Lily took the phone. ''Mel, if Wayman is on that boat with Susie, he has men on it, too,'' Lily said. ''I have a better idea.''

Mel didn't like the sound of that.

''Let me go on board. I can distract him and his men. I'll give you a signal indicating how many. Then you can call for backup and rescue all of us.''

''No.''

There was no way in hell Mel was going to let Lily on the boat, not for any reason. He might not agree with the actions Lily and Susie had taken, but he had come full circle to believe that Wayman Bishop was capable of terrible violence.

''It's best for me to go. If Wayman sees me, he'll know that he's been caught. He'll realize that he can't possibly continue. With you, he might shoot you before you get a chance to open your mouth.''

''No he won't. He'll have to gloat first.''

Mel could see Lily's profile in the moonlight, and suddenly he knew that her opinion of violent men was based on personal experience, not conjecture. He said nothing, but he vowed that whoever had hurt Lily in such a way would pay for it—and sooner rather than later.

"Lily, you're not..." He realized he was on the wrong track. "I don't want you to go on the boat. Please, let's do it my way."

"Because it's the best way, or the safest way for me?" she asked.

He couldn't help but grin. She was quick on her feet. "If you're safe, I can devote all of my focus to tending to business. If I have to be worried about what's happening to you, I put myself in more danger."

She gave him a long look. "You're too smart to be a man," she said, smiling to take the sting out of her words. "That's a compliment."

He could resist no longer. His arm went around her and drew her gently into his chest. "You have a lot to learn about men, Lily. Some men, at least. And I have a lot to learn about women. I think we can teach each other some pretty important things."

Her hands went to his shoulders and then around his neck. "Mel, promise that if you walk onto that boat, you'll come back to teach me those things." She closed her eyes, but a tear trickled slowly down her cheek. "I want to learn about you."

Mel lowered his face, letting his lips brush lightly across her soft cheek. Her salty tears were the sweetest thing he'd ever tasted. "With you waiting for me, the devil couldn't keep me from coming back," he said before he kissed her.

The feel of Lily in his arms, responding to his kiss, was better than any fantasy he'd ever concocted. Mel had never bought into the once-in-a-lifetime-love theory, but as he deepened his kiss, he knew he'd been wrong. Chances were that he'd been wrong about a lot of things. As soon as Susie and the baby were safe and Wayman Bishop was behind bars, Mel intended to spend some time evaluating his beliefs. And Lily would be at his side to help him.

He gently ended the kiss. "See that window?" he asked, pointing. He knew by the design of the boat that it was likely a den or party space on the main deck. "Watch for me there. When I'm ready, I'll wave to you, twice. That's the signal to radio for backup."

"I can do that," Lily said.

"You can do anything, lady." He knew he had to go without further delay. It was getting harder by the second to think of leaving Lily behind in possible danger. Mel knew that just because Susie and the infant were likely on the boat, there was no guarantee that Lily was safe on land. "Be careful," he whispered. "There could be men out here."

"Go," she said, her voice breaking.

Mel darted into the darkness, but as he ran lightly down the pier toward the boat, his body was clearly visible in the bright moonlight.

WHILE THE BIPEDS were spooning and sparring, I did a little reconnaissance. Not much to find on this end of the pier, except a lot of tire marks. This has been one busy place in the last few hours.

I'm not so certain I like this setup. Margie Lavert was awfully forthcoming with all the information about the boat and the marina. Of course, she is a cop's widow, and detail is a way of life for those in law enforcement. I guess it was Clotilde who picked up on her perfect cooperation.

I have highly trained observing skills, but Clotilde has a double dose of acute observation—feline and female. It's difficult to concede, but sometimes she's just a little more astute than even I. Which puts her about a million light years ahead of humanoids.

She couldn't put her finger on exactly what it was about the grieving widow, but she got vibes. And not the good ones either.

Now I have a choice. Should I follow Dick Tracy up to the boat and protect him, or should I stay here with the girls? Given a choice between girls and detectives, girls, normally, would win out hands down. If only I could subdivide like an amoeba and be in two places at once.

I'll ask Clotilde what I should do. She'll certainly have an opinion. I don't know a female who doesn't.

Wait a minute! What's that noise? Thunderation! It's a car coming. Run, Lily, run! She's hiding deeper in the foliage, which I guess is the best thing to do. There's no way she can make it back to the car. The parking area is wide-open and the arriving car has headlights sweeping the asphalt as if the driver knew to look for us.

As if the driver knew... Holy! Moly! Clotilde was right! It's Margie Lavert and a couple of big thugs.

And they came right here. That witch sent us here and then followed us. We're trapped like rats on a sinking ship. There's nowhere for Lily to run, and Mel is on the ship already.

Damn! He's in the window giving the signal. He wants backup! And Lily can't do a thing but hold her breath and pray Margie and her beefed-up muscle service don't see her.

Oh, no! Mrs. Evil-Eye Lavert spotted Lily. Smart girl, she's not trying to run. She's standing up as cool as a cucumber.

They're ordering Lily down the pier. The thugs are looking for Mel, but it won't take them long to figure out that he's on the boat. The best thing is for me and Clotilde to lay low and try to figure out a plan of attack. If Lily is with Mel, he'll protect her. Now's the time I could really use human language. I don't think the radio dispatcher would understand cat talk.

Okay, Lily, just be cool. Do what they say. That's a good girl. She's coming out of the shrubs.

No, Lily, don't raise the gun! Good grief! Clotilde is rushing into the fray! No! Clotilde, don't jump on him! Oh! he's firing at Clotilde! She's running. Run, baby, run hard! I have to make sure she wasn't hit.

The other one tackled Lily. The gun went flying! They've got Lily now, and none too gently. They're headed to the boat, and I have to find my lady love. What a fiasco!

Chapter Fifteen

Lily brushed the grit from her hands. Her palms were raw from her tumble on the asphalt, and her body ached from the bruises inflicted by one of the men who'd arrived with Margie Lavert. Worst of all, she'd lost the gun Mel had given her—and any hope she might have had of averting capture.

"That wasn't smart," Margie Lavert said calmly. "Now move along. I'm sure Wayman will be glad to see you."

Lily stumbled as one of the men pushed her down the pier. She looked back. The gallant little calico had tried to help her. She could only hope that in the darkness the man hadn't been able to shoot the cat. Familiar had been smart enough to stay hidden.

"You won't get away with this," Lily said.

"Don't count on it. Where's the cop?"

Lily didn't answer and felt a push at her back. "I don't know," she said. "He left me here to watch the boat."

"And he left on foot?" Margie laughed. "Right."

Lily could only hope that the gunfire had alerted

Mel. Maybe he was hiding on the boat, waiting to ambush Margie and her minions when they went on board.

Her slim hope was shattered when she was pushed into the cabin. Mel sat in a chair. Standing behind him with a gun at his head was Wayman Bishop.

"Lily!" Susie Bishop sat in a corner with the baby on her lap. She burst into tears. "He's going to kill all of us," she cried.

"I don't think so," Lily said calmly, though she was absolutely terrified. She saw from Mel's expression that he approved of her tact.

"He's going to kill all of us and take the baby," Susie insisted, crying louder.

"Shut up," Wayman said, swinging the gun in her direction. "Shut up, or I'll do it now."

Susie wisely swallowed back her tears. She began rocking back and forth, huddling over her baby.

Lily exchanged a glance with Mel. He was sitting quietly, but he was far from defeated. She could see it in his eyes. He turned to Margie.

"This is unexpected," he said conversationally. "I should have suspected."

"Yes, you should have." Margie Lavert went to stand beside Wayman. "Can we possibly get rid of all of them?"

"Easily," he said, smiling.

He reminded Lily of a shark. He was three-piece-suit smooth, a model of grooming and power. But he was all predator. No wonder Susie was terrified of him.

"I wouldn't be so sure. My boss isn't easy to fool," Lily said. "You can't just murder three more people and think you'll walk out of this with the baby."

"You forget, Lily. I'm the man with the mayor's ear. It isn't that hard to arrange a scenario where you three die, say, in a fire. Or in a car wreck. My story is airtight. You and Susie were in cahoots to rob me of my child. Our very earnest police detective stumbled upon the two of you and attempted to bring you to justice. In the end, unfortunately, you all died." His smile was the cruelest thing Lily had ever seen.

"It won't work." Lily was bluffing, but she had to. She knew from experience with her ex-brother-in-law that the worst thing she could do was show fear. A man like Wayman Bishop fed off the fear of others. "Three bodies together! Forget it. The paper will launch an investigation. I've left notes in the office. Notes that implicate you as an abuser."

Lily clenched her fists at her side. She hadn't actually left notes. But it was the only card she had to play.

Wayman's eyes narrowed and his mouth became a grim line. He looked at the two men who'd come in with Margie. "Her apartment. The newspaper office. Find those notes. If you have any trouble, we can get a court order for the search."

The men left without another word.

"You see, Lily, it's convenient being the mayor's right-hand man. I have power that you can't imagine. If I want something, I simply order it."

"The newspaper won't allow a search. You may

have power, but not enough to bulldoze over the First Amendment. You'll be tied up in court for years, and my boss will nail you to the wall. Think about it, Bishop. If you go in there demanding my notes and I turn up dead, where does that point the finger of suspicion?''

Wayman Bishop laughed out loud. "I'll make sure it points at our detective, here," he said easily. "Keep talking, Lily. Every time you open your mouth, you tell me another loose end to tie up.''

Lily gritted her teeth. What he said was true. The best thing she could do was shut up.

Margie walked over to Wayman and began to rub his shoulders. "Maybe we shouldn't kill them right now," she said softly. "Maybe we should wait until we see what she's written.''

Wayman shrugged out from under her hands and turned to glare at her. "Maybe you should leave the thinking to me," he barked. "I've been damn good at it for the past two years. We got rid of your husband, didn't we?''

Margie's smile trembled. "Okay, honey. I was just trying to be helpful.''

"Well don't." He paced across the room. "Get the baby's things, Susie.''

"No!" She bent over the infant, using her body as a block to protect him.

"You stupid little fool!" Wayman walked to her and snatched her hair, jerking her head backward. "Don't make me teach you another lesson. I don't have time to use the caution I need to keep from breaking up that face of yours again.''

''No!'' Lily cried.

Mel started out of his seat, but Wayman swung the gun on him. ''Give me a reason, Haskin.'' He waited until Mel was seated again.

''Now, Susie.'' He jerked her hair one more time. ''Get the baby's things and get ready to go. You're coming with me.''

''Wayman,'' Susie cried, her voice trembling with fear and pain. ''Why don't—''

At the look he gave her she stopped in mid sentence.

''Let's go.'' Wayman hauled Susie to her feet. ''Give me one reason and I'll give your friend Lily a little of what you need.''

''Okay, okay.'' Susie began picking up the diaper bag and other supplies with quick, jerky motions.

''Watch her,'' Wayman ordered Margie. He pointed the gun at Mel and Lily. ''You two, out the door. There's a storage room on the boat where you can spend a few hours. I'd use it wisely. You know, confess your sins or whatever. When I come back you're going to be toast.''

Lily felt as if she were walking to her grave as she led the way down the darkened, narrow passage on the boat. The vessel was bigger than she'd thought, and it was clear as she and Mel were forced down a steep set of narrow stairs that they were going below the water level. In fact, the shush of the water against the hull was ominous and terrifying.

She felt Mel's hand brush her back and knew that he was trying to offer her comfort. But the truth was, they were going to die together.

"Easy, Lily," Mel's whisper caressed her.

"Shut up," Wayman ordered. "One more word from you, Haskin, and I'll put a bullet in your friend's leg."

Lily kept walking. She could almost feel the lead penetrating her back, but she kept her posture stiff and did her best not to show how afraid she really was.

When they came to a steel door, Wayman ordered her to open it. She did, revealing only darkness. She didn't have long to look. Wayman pushed Mel, who stumbled into her. Together they went crashing to the hard metal floor as she heard the door slam behind them. There was the sound of the lock sliding into place.

No longer under pressure to keep up a brave front, Lily felt a sob rising in her throat. The fear tore at her as she tried to hold it back.

Mel's arms pulled her close, and she thought she'd never felt anything so safe and steady as his hard body. There was a click and a tiny flame leaped to life in his hand. The cigarette lighter gave them enough illumination to examine their prison.

The room was a twelve-foot square with no windows. The only entrance was the door they'd been pushed through. A mattress covered with a thin blanket was on the floor, and beside it a baby bottle. Obviously this had been Susie's prison, too. At least for a little while.

With an oath, Mel let the lighter go out. He carefully maneuvered Lily to the mattress in the darkness and helped her down. In a moment he was beside her, pulling her to lean against him as he braced on the wall.

"I have a confession to make," Mel said softly in her ear.

It was the last thing Lily expected to hear, and just as she knew Mel intended, it gave her a chance to get a grip on her emotions. "What?" she asked, her voice still shaky.

"I was dead wrong," he said, his hands moving over her arms and back, comforting, soothing.

"About what?" She felt a little steadier.

"About Susie and the baby. I would have given my child away to keep him out of the hands of Wayman Bishop. I would have done exactly what she did. You were right to help her, Lily. I only wish I'd listened to you sooner. Maybe we wouldn't be in this position if I hadn't been so hardheaded."

Lily leaned her head against his chest. His heartbeat was strong, steady, a lifeline to living. Twelve hours before she would have danced a jig at Mel's confession. Now, she realized that it mattered, but only to her. The course of events couldn't be changed.

"Thank you for saying it," she said.

"Once we're out of here, I'll work with you to help Susie. Wayman is going to spend the rest of his life in prison, I can promise you that. Susie will be safe. She won't have to give up her baby."

Lily closed her eyes and tried to hold on to that

image—Susie in the park with little David as he grew from infant to toddler. It was a beautiful picture, but the hard reality was that if Susie wasn't already dead, she would be in a matter of hours. Just as they would.

"What was the shooting about?" Mel asked. "When I heard the gunfire, I thought I would die."

"They were shooting at Clotilde. She attacked one of Margie's men. I only hope she got away."

"And Familiar?" Mel asked with a hint of hope in his voice.

"He's out there," Lily said, her own hope also rising, then plummeting. "What can he do? He's out in the middle of nowhere and he can't drive and he can't talk."

Mel squeezed her tight. "This case has taught me two extremely valuable lessons. One is that I can't judge another's actions by my past. The other is never to underestimate those cats."

"I've learned some things, too," Lily said. Her palm rested on Mel's chest, just above his heart.

"I don't think this is the kind of confession Wayman had in mind for us," Mel said.

Lily could have kissed him for his bravado and attempts to raise her spirits. "Perhaps not, but I want to tell you this, Mel. I let my past interfere, too. My sister's violent marriage to a policeman made me prejudge you. I was wrong." She gave a weak laugh. "Dead wrong."

"Not quite that wrong," Mel said.

"How long do you think we have?" Lily asked. She knew Mel wouldn't lie to her.

"A couple of hours."

"Then I think we should make the best use of our time," she said softly.

There was the sharp intake of his breath. She didn't wait for more encouragement. She lifted her face and kissed his cheek, moving her lips unerringly to his lips.

In the darkness, Lily felt no constraints or shyness. Her fingers sought the buttons of his shirt as she felt his hands moving over her body, loosening the blouse she wore, pulling it from her slacks.

The boat rocked ever so gently on the river as Mel eased her down to the mattress and followed her, his lips claiming hers with increasing passion.

Lily lost herself in the wonder of Mel's touch. Desperation made each sensation more intense, and in the darkness of her prison, she acknowledged that she'd fallen deeply in love with Mel.

He took such care with her. His hands and lips appraised every inch of her body, and Lily reciprocated. Her palms drifted over the muscles of his chest, the flatness of his abdomen. He was physical perfection, and the beauty of his body was only more apparent in the darkness beneath her hands.

"Mel," she whispered, catching his hands with hers and holding him still for a moment.

"Yes," he said, his voice rough with passion.

"I have to tell you something."

He freed one hand from her grip and gently found her cheek. "Tell me."

"It's just that we might never get another chance, and I want you to know."

"Go ahead," he encouraged.

"I love you," she said.

His palm caressed her cheek. "So brave," he whispered. "Will you regret those words when we walk out of here?"

She trembled at the hope in his words. "No," she answered. "And I promise that I'll try to live the rest of my life without ever again regretting what I feel for you."

"Ah, Lily. I've loved you since the moment you infuriated me," he said, his voice rich with humor and love.

"Think of the time we've wasted," she said.

"Let's just use the time we have." He brought his lips to hers and Lily forgot about time or danger or anything except for the man she'd given her heart to.

THE BAD GUYS have abandoned ship, but they've taken Susie and the baby. Clotilde, thank goodness, is perfectly fine. Just a tiny chunk of tail hair missing where one bullet came very close. Too close. Those humanoids are going to pay big time for that shooting spree.

I have to say, though, that my lady love has nerves of steel. She's far less upset about it than I am. All she wants to do is figure out how to find Mel and Lily.

They have to be on the boat. And I didn't hear any gunshots, so I'm assuming they're alive. Of course there are always knives and strangulation, a point I won't raise to Clotilde just at the moment.

She's right. We have to find Mel and Lily and then get hot on the trail of Susie and the baby.

Eureka! I have an idea. I can't talk human talk, but what if we go to the car and turn the radio on. Surely that would signal the police that something has happened to Mel.

Clotilde thinks it's a good idea. My attitude is, it couldn't hurt. Chop! Chop! Clotilde. Let's get this done and then head for the boat.

When this is over, I want a huge platter of fried shrimp. I'm talking at least three dozen. And I want crab claws and a dish of fresh cream. I'll just keep my mind focused on that and away from the dire possibilities of what we might find on the boat.

Okay, the radio is off the hook. I'm pressing the call button. There's the dispatcher. She's sounding annoyed that I don't respond. If only she knew. There has to be a way to wedge this button down. Right, Clotilde. I'll brace it in the seat against the seat-belt hook. Perfect. Now if they can only trace this signal, we might have some help before it's too late.

MEL HELD LILY in his arms, delighting in the way she slept against him. She was some woman. He was glad that she'd found a few moments of forgetfulness in sleep. He, too, was exhausted, but his mind wouldn't shut down.

With all of his immediate problems at hand, he kept going back to the past. To his own childhood. He kept seeing himself standing in the hallway of the orphanage as his mother walked away. Only this time, he heard her sobs as she hurried away from him. Odd how he'd never remembered that she'd been crying, and that she'd run the last few steps to the door on a burst of awful tears.

Was it possible that she hadn't wanted to leave him? That maybe it was the best choice she had?

He sighed, wondering what the truth might be. The better question was, did it even matter anymore? Mel knew then that he'd at last forgiven his mother for leaving him. It was about time. The strangest thing of all was that in forgiving her, he'd opened the door of his own self-made prison.

"Thank you, Lily," he said, bending low to kiss her forehead.

She stirred in his arms and he shifted so that she rested more comfortably.

How long had they been locked in? It was almost impossible to calculate the passage of time in the dark. Would he hear Wayman Bishop when he returned, or would he simply find himself on a burning boat? Mel had tried to keep up a brave front for Lily. In reality, though, he believed that they could die.

"Mel?" Lily's voice was groggy with sleep.

"Yes," he said, amazed at how just her voice could make him want her again with such intensity.

"Don't leave me," she said.

"Never," he answered, pulling the blanket up over her naked body. It seemed that the room had grown cooler. Probably because the temperature had dropped during the night.

He leaned his head against the hard wall and tried to come up with a plan. The horror that lingered at the back of his thoughts was that Wayman Bishop could simply leave them on the boat. In a few days they'd die of thirst. It wasn't the kind of death Mel wanted, especially not for Lily. But then with Wayman's influence, it wouldn't be hard to have such a couple of deaths ruled accidental.

He tried to put that out of his mind. He was trying to focus on whether he'd left any usable clues on his desk when he heard the soft scratch at the door.

The scratch came again, followed by a soft mewling sound. The walls were thick, and Mel couldn't be sure, but he gently roused Lily.

"Listen," he whispered as she slowly came awake.

"What?"

"Just listen. Tell me what you hear."

The scratching came again, followed by the muted cry.

Lily sat straight up. "It's Familiar!" she said, hope surging in her voice. "That cat! He's out there trying to rescue us."

"I doubt even Familiar can open the door," Mel pointed out. "It's one of those locking systems. Wayman isn't stupid. If there was a chance we could get out, he would have left a guard."

"I thought you weren't going to underestimate the cat," Lily said. She was wide-awake and crawling across the floor to the door.

"Familiar," she said, leaning down so that her lips were close to the crack at the bottom of the door. "We're in here. Get help."

"Meow!"

Mel distinctly heard the cat. If Familiar could somehow get him and Lily out of the room, they might actually stand a chance of making an escape.

"Get help," Mel said, moving across the floor to join Lily.

"Meow," came another cry.

"It's Clotilde," Lily said. "Thank goodness she's okay. I was afraid they might have shot her."

"You two get a move on it. Get us some help," Mel said. "Whatever it takes, I know you'll figure it out. Just please hurry. I'm afraid our minutes are numbered."

Chapter Sixteen

Lily drew on her clothes, having some difficulty in the dark. Her things were tangled with Mel's, and it took trial and error to find the right articles of clothing. With Familiar and Clotilde's appearance, Lily felt the first real hope that they might be saved.

"He'll get us out of this," Mel said, echoing Lily's thoughts.

"I believe he will," Lily agreed. "I just don't want to be naked when the posse arrives to save us."

Mel settled his arms around her. "Please tell me that I won't have to get us locked in a room before I can make love to you again."

"I promise. Locking me in a room will never be necessary," Lily said. She kissed him and found herself wanting much more. Reluctantly she eased back. "Mel, whatever else happens, we can't let what we feel for each other slip away from us."

"I don't think we could run from it," Mel said. "Now let's talk about what happens next. No matter who opens that door, you remain back here. I'll rush out and take down as many as I can. Then you come out and make a dash for freedom.''

''I'm not leaving you,'' Lily said indignantly.

''If you escape, it wouldn't do them any good to kill me. You might actually be my lifeline.''

''Then you run and leave me behind. You'll stand a better chance of getting away.'' Lily knew her argument was valid. She also knew that Mel would ignore it.

''Lily, you're smart, but you're also a torment. Just this once, please do as I ask.''

''Just this once,'' she agreed with some doubt.

A noise outside the door got her attention. ''Listen.'' She couldn't positively identify the noise, but it sounded as if the cats were shifting furniture.

''I hope they hurry,'' Mel said.

Lily agreed, completely. At any moment Wayman Bishop could decide to finish them off. Still, the best thing she and Mel could do was to relax as much as possible. She was as tense as a coiled spring. When they did get out, she'd need all of her strength and stamina. No point in exhausting herself now.

''Mel, can I ask you something?'' She reached in the darkness until she found his hand.

''Sure,'' he said, his fingers traveling up her arm to finally circle her torso and draw her back into his embrace.

''Why does the idea of an abandoned baby upset you so? I mean, I could guess that it has something to do with your own childhood. But I don't want to guess. I want to know the absolute truth.''

There was a long silence. Lily could also easily assume that Mel didn't talk about his past or personal demons very often. She was asking a lot of him.

"When I was four my mother took me to St. Anthony's Orphanage. It was the darkest place I'd ever been, and I was terrified. Walking down the hallway, our footsteps echoed. Hers went click click in her high heels. I remember it perfectly, those short, rapid steps.

"I thought it was a doctor's office or a hospital, some place like that where we were going to visit Grandma."

Lily held perfectly still. Mel unconsciously moved his hands up and down her arms, offering her the comfort he had so badly needed as a child.

"My grandmother had been very sick, and I guess in the back of my mind I was afraid we were going to find her dead. That seemed like the perfect place for a dead person—so dark and hollow. Like a coffin, or at least how a four-year-old imagines a coffin."

Lily shifted so that she could touch his face. She simply let her palm caress his cheek, encouraging him.

"Anyway, the upshot was that we talked to this woman for a while, and then my mother stood up and kissed me on the head. Tears were running down her face, but she didn't make a sound. She just walked out of the room."

Lily felt her own tears threaten, but she swallowed them back. Mel needed to keep talking, to get it all out at last.

"I ran after her, but by the time I got to the hallway, she was way ahead. She was walking fast, and then she was running. She was sobbing and running, and she pushed open the heavy door and ran out into the sunlight. The door slammed and I never saw her again.''

Lily sighed. There were no words that would help, nothing that would undo the pain that Mel had suffered as a child.

"I always assumed she didn't want the responsibility, that she got tired of taking care of a kid. My father, I suppose, abandoned us or something. I never knew.''

"Have you ever made an attempt to find your mother?" Lily asked gently.

"Until today, I always thought she was a selfish woman. I had no desire to try and find her.''

"And now?" Lily asked.

"I don't know," Mel said slowly. "I don't know if it would be better or worse to actually learn the truth. What I do know for certain now is that it doesn't matter nearly as much. Whatever her reasons were for leaving me, I grew up in that orphanage with plenty to eat and a good education. That's a lot more than some kids who have two parents get.''

Lily kissed his cheek. "Mel, you're a remarkable man. I don't know if you realize how hard it is to forgive the unforgivable.''

"And you, Lily? Can you forgive?" Mel asked.

Lily gave a soft chuckle. "I don't know if I can ever forgive Bobby Reynolds for nearly killing my sister and beating her until she had to have a hysterectomy. Maybe I can't forgive him, but I can forgive Babs.''

"Your sister?" Mel asked, surprised.

"Yes. She's the one I need to forgive. For loving someone who hurt her." Lily kissed his cheek again. "See, I've learned some things, too. I've been furious with Babs for being so foolish as to stay with someone for so long who could inflict such pain and damage on her. Because of that, I've kept myself from loving anyone—for fear I would be as stupid as I'd judged her to be."

Mel's strong hands rubbed her back, encouraging her to continue.

"Bobby isn't the problem. My own fear is. That's what I've finally had to confront."

"Oh, Lily." Mel pulled her close. "I thought grown-ups were supposed to be smart and wise and all of that. What happened to us?"

"You only get to be smart and wise if you put the past in its proper perspective, Mel."

"Then promise me one thing," Mel said. "When we get out of this room, we no longer let our pasts control the present. And that's where we're going to live. No past, no future—just what we have right at the moment."

"Now that's a challenge I'll accept," Lily agreed.

There was a loud slam and an angry cat yowl.

"Whatever they're doing, they're working hard," Mel said.

Lily crossed her fingers in the dark. "Familiar is capable of anything. You said it, Mel. We just have to believe it." She felt his lips at her neck.

"And we have to believe in each other," he whispered against her skin.

IT WAS CLOTILDE'S brilliant idea to shove that box over here so that I could stand on it and lasso the dead bolt with this telephone cord. Yes, it's the work of a genius mind. The problem is that the dang box keeps tilting because this wretched ship is shifting with the current.

Water is not an element to be trusted. There's a reason cats have a natural aversion to it. It looks solid, but isn't. It can be more forceful than a rock, and yet it's fluid. It can freeze or evaporate. There's absolutely nothing stable about it. And now it's lifting and dropping this boat in a rhythm just irregular enough so that I can't time my lasso to drop over the thumb bolt like it should.

And then I fall off the box. And Clotilde laughs. I didn't laugh when she was almost getting shot. Females! They can certainly get a fella's hair up.

She says that it's always funny when a cat falls. It has to do with our natural dignity, she says. Humph! I don't find it amusing at all. It isn't my dignity that's hurting, it's my backside where I landed. And we're no closer to freeing Mel and Lily.

Ah, that got her little feline attention. I have to remember that this is Clotilde's first case. It's probably better if she doesn't understand how dire the situation is. Ol' Wayman could return at any minute. Then it would be curtains for Mel and Lily. Not to mention Susie. So let's make one more attempt at this thumb bolt. If it doesn't work this time, we'll have to think up a new approach.

Okay, I'm on the box. Tottering on the edge, I might add. I sling the telephone cord, which is a neat trick since I have to use my mouth. And there it goes, sailing up, up, up—and onto the dead bolt. Eureka!

So I've won Clotilde's admiration at last. Well, it was a long, hard battle. Now I have to ease this cord tighter until…there it is. I've got it!

Clotilde is going to help me pull. Gently, my dear. I have to sort of wiggle the hammer of the thumb bolt down. Wayman is no fool, but he didn't figure that Mel and Lily would have two loyal friends just waiting to help them escape.

There it goes. Now I'll just have to leap on the lever of a handle and force it down in the hopes that Lily and Mel are paying enough attention so that when the lock clicks, they'll move fast and push the door open. Otherwise, they won't get out.

What? Clotilde hears something. With this dratted boat shifting and rocking, I didn't hear a thing. Of course, the water is making all sorts of noises all around us.

Clotilde insists it's something against the hull of the boat. Probably a shark, just waiting for a little kitty paw to hang off in the water. Snap! A three-legged kitty is the end result. Or maybe piranhas. They're probably battering their tiny, deadly little bodies against the hull because they can smell me in here.

Oh, no. Clotilde says it's worse than piranhas. It's

Wayman. He and his men are climbing on board right this minute.

Hang on, Mel and Lily. Here comes rescue. One long leap! I grab the lever and let my weight force it down. There's the click, and I feel the door moving. Yes, Mel is pushing it open. Hey! Not so hard. You're going to knock me into a wall!

Well, look at that. Just like a show-off. He comes out in a somersault, rolls to his feet, crouched like a sprinter, and he's ready for action. Too bad Wayman is ready for action, too. And Clotilde is warning Mel. So I guess my job is to check on Lily. Tough duty, eh?

MEL SAW THE CALICO and knew by her arched back and hissing that something was wrong. It had to be the bad guys. And he didn't have a weapon.

"Lily, come on." She moved up behind him, and Mel glanced down at Familiar at her side.

"They're out there," he whispered to her.

"How many?"

He shook his head. The hallway in front of him had several doors. He took Lily's hand and they moved silently toward the first one. Mel pushed it open. The bedroom was small, and there was no exit. He moved on to the next door. When he opened it, he saw that it was a study. He wasn't certain it was a good choice, but he had to take it. He could hear footsteps coming his way.

He and Lily and the cats eased into the room and shut the door. He didn't have to tell Familiar and Clotilde to find a hiding place. The two cats instantly disappeared in the dark room.

Crossing the room, he pushed open a door. There was a small bathroom. And no exit.

"We have to go up," he said. "There won't be any windows until we get on the deck level." If only he'd had more time to study the layout of the boat. The only stairwell he knew would most likely lead him straight into Wayman's hands.

"They're coming." Lily swung to face the door.

Mel stepped in front of her, relieved to hear the footsteps pass by them. In a matter of seconds, there was the cry of outrage. Wayman had discovered their escape.

In a dark corner of the room was an armoire. It wasn't the best hiding place, but Mel hoped that Wayman would assume they were off the boat. If they did a cursory search, they might not think of the armoire.

"Quick." He pulled Lily toward the furniture, opened the door and helped her settle inside. There was hardly room for her long legs.

"I'm not staying here without you," Lily said.

"Remember," Mel leaned closer and kissed her as he covered her in the blankets stored in the bottom of the piece, "I'm more effective if you're safe. So try and stay safe."

"No, I—"

"Lily, please."

He saw fear in her green eyes, but he also saw love. She bit her bottom lip and nodded. "Okay."

Just as he was about to close the door, the little

calico cat jumped into the armoire with her. He looked down and saw Familiar at his side.

"Give Clotilde some pats. And trust me," Mel said gently. "I'll be back. I promise."

"You'd better not shatter my newfound trust in men, Mel Haskin," Lily said, fighting back tears.

He closed the door and patted it once for luck. If she was quiet, she might be okay. The armoire was barely big enough to hold a child. Perhaps she would be safely hidden.

He left the room, Familiar at his heels. He checked the hallway and then darted into it. He could try and take Bishop out, or he could make an attempt to get to the police car and try to radio for help. Mel personally favored an attack on Wayman, but his common sense told him that the radio was the best bet. With backup, Lily wouldn't be in as much danger.

He found the steps that led to the deck and slowly eased up them. At last he could see the night sky, a velvety black with a scattering of stars. He could also hear the wind, a low breeze that built to a gust and then settled down again. It sounded as if a storm were brewing.

Mel advanced, lifting his eyes above the deck level and scanning the empty area around him. There was no sign of Wayman or his men. And Susie? What had Wayman done with her? Mel's anger boiled as he thought of the way Wayman had snatched her hair and hauled her around.

"Hello, Mel."

The low female voice was completely calm.

Mel turned into the barrel of a big handgun. Margie Levert was holding the weapon.

"So all the little rats are coming out to play. Where's that reporter?"

"I don't know." Whatever he said, Mel knew it might tip them that Lily was still on the ship. In the darkness he couldn't make out Margie's features, just the huge black bore of the gun.

"I hope she's not on this ship," Margie said. "Then again, it might be for the best for both of you. I've come to a full appreciation of what it means to be female and the recipient of Wayman's ire."

She lit a cigarette, and in the brief flare of the lighter, Mel saw the black eye that was nearly swollen shut.

"Good grief," he said on an intake of breath. "What happened to you?"

"Oh, I'm the clumsy kind. I must have fallen-hit-a-door-or-tripped." She inhaled deeply, making the tip of her cigarette glow. "Isn't that what women in my situation say?"

"I don't think you're required to stay in that situation." Mel felt a glimmer of hope. "I mean, you haven't really done anything, have you?"

"Does wishing my husband dead count?"

Mel hesitated. "Wishing isn't against the law. Taking action to accomplish such a goal is." He paused. "But you know that already, don't you?"

"Jim dug his own grave," Margie said. "He sold out to Wayman lock, stock and barrel a long time ago.

And then, when he got frustrated because of something Wayman wanted him to do, he took it out on me.''

"So you moved from Jim to Wayman?'' Mel almost couldn't believe the irony of her choice.

"I figured if I was going to get hit, I could get hit by someone who could make it worth my while.'' She laughed, a hard, grating sound.

"Was it worth what it cost you?''

"Hardly,'' Margie said, laughing softly to herself. "That's the problem here. I'm no better at making financial choices than I ever was at romantic choices. Somehow it seems I always pick the wrong one.''

Mel saw an opportunity and wondered if Margie had deliberately opened the door. "You don't have to go down with the wrong choice. If you weren't involved in killing Jim, then we might be able to work out a deal.''

He almost yelped in surprise. Familiar was on the stairs beside him and had bitten his leg, hard. He controlled his reaction, though, and focused on Margie. He was winning her over. He was sure of it. She might actually help him.

"Oh, yeah? What good will a deal do me when you're dead?'' she asked.

"Think about it, Margie. Let me go. It's only a matter of time until you're caught. Lily will have notified the authorities by now. Sure, maybe Wayman will kill me. What's one more to his list of crimes? But so far, you don't have blood on your hands.''

The gun shook in her hand and Mel was about to

make a lunge for it when he heard something click behind his ear.

"Well, well, well, Detective Haskin. I was beginning to fear that you'd gotten off the boat."

Mel swung around to face Wayman and his 38-caliber pistol.

"He says the reporter is gone," Margie reported.

"Yes, that's what he says. But he's still here, isn't he? For some reason that makes me believe she might still be here, too. That would be so much more convenient."

Wayman reached toward him, and Mel caught the distinct whiff of gasoline on his hands.

"What are you doing?" Mel asked.

"Oh, just setting up another perfect crime. Follow me up on the deck. Margie, make sure he does."

Mel slowly ascended the remaining steps, following Wayman, and stood on the deck. He looked around. The shoreline was as empty as it had been when he'd first arrived.

"Where's Susie and the baby?" Mel asked, dreading to hear the answer.

"Oh, Susie's still alive, if that's what you're worried about. She's in a safe place and minding my son. She seems quite content to do so. You know, she would have been a really terrific mother, if she'd only listened to reason."

Mel didn't bother to respond. He started walking toward the well-lit room that Wayman indicated.

"Have a seat," Wayman said, indicating a plush leather sofa.

As Mel sat down he turned to face Margie. He wasn't successful at hiding his shock. Her face was battered, and though she'd tried to clean the blood away, she'd missed several places.

"Make him stop staring at me," Margie said, putting a hand up to shield the damage to her face.

"Where are your manners, Detective?" Wayman asked. "Margie is ashamed that she had to be punished. You shouldn't stare at her."

Mel looked away from Margie and at Wayman. "I just don't know which one of you is the craziest," he said.

"That really isn't your concern. Lily should be the focus of your anxiety," Wayman said casually. He yelled out the door and the two thugs reappeared. "Tear this ship apart and find that woman."

"She's gone," Mel said. "And you're running out of time."

"Then maybe I should just shoot you now and be done with it. As you so aptly told Margie, I've already got blood on my hands. What's one more?"

Wayman lifted the handgun, pointed it at Mel's heart and cocked the hammer.

Chapter Seventeen

Lily pressed herself against the wall of the stairwell and forced herself to remain steady. She could hear the conversation and knew that Mel's life hung in the balance. He was a prisoner, held at gunpoint by a man who could batter his wife or kill in the blink of an eye, while in the rooms below, two hired guns were hunting for her.

"Meow." Familiar hooked a claw in the leg of her slacks and urged her to remain still.

Lily held her breath and listened to the conversation on the deck.

"Go ahead and shoot me," Mel said. "Put Margie in line for a charge of capital murder, too. That's what will happen, Margie. You may have been a victim in the past, but you're a part of it now."

"Wait a minute, Wayman," Margie said. Her voice was pleading.

Lily exhaled softly. She had to think! What to do? And where were Susie and the baby? Whatever action Lily took would impact on all of them. There was no room for errors.

Beside her, Clotilde eased forward to the top of the stairs. Familiar joined her. Both cats crept onto the deck. She eased her head up to look and saw them dart into the shadows by the cabin where Mel was being held.

"Margie, I'm warning you to stay out of this," Wayman said. "I don't need a woman telling me what to do."

"This is my life you're jeopardizing," Margie said.

"Do we need to have another little discussion?" Wayman asked with an edge of anger in his voice.

Lily gritted her teeth. Wayman was the same kind of man as Bobby Reynolds. A bully and a sadist. And judging by the conversation she'd heard, he was contemplating shooting the man she loved.

"No, Wayman," Margie said in a meeker tone. "But let's think this through. If you shoot him, it's murder and the police won't let it go. You know how they are when one of their own is killed. You've already killed one cop. This will be impossible for them to look away from, no matter how much power you have." Her voice softened, taking on a coaxing tone. "But if we go on with the plan you had, you know, setting the boat on fire, it'll look like an accident. Just knock him out and let's get this over with."

Lily felt her panic increase. She had to act. Easing up on deck she crouched low to the wall of the cabin where the cats waited. Peeping in a window she saw the scene—Mel in a chair with Wayman standing over him, gun pointed right at his head. Her first instinct was to rush into the room and charge Wayman, but she knew that would only make matters worse. She couldn't let her feelings for Mel blind her to the further danger her actions might produce. Looking for an alternative plan, she saw Margie to the left, pacing.

"Yeow!" Familiar's voice was low, growling. Clotilde's response was in the same vein, only more feminine.

Lily tore her eyes away from Mel and focused on the cats. Something was going on with them. They were both arched and spitting, tails twitching. To her horror, she heard the two thugs below deck.

"She's not down here. Let's check up top."

She glanced around the deck, searching for a hiding place. Clotilde scampered toward what seemed to be the wheelhouse. Familiar rushed to the boat's railing and began batting the ropes with a paw.

"Brilliant!" Lily said, realizing what the cats wanted. She hurried to Familiar and quickly untied the boat. If the boat were loose, at least one of the men would be occupied trying to get it back to the dock. It would also prevent any of Wayman's reinforcements from boarding.

Tossing the lines to the pier she ran to the wheelhouse. The key to the engines dangled in place. She'd never started a boat in her life, but she knew she had to do it now. Trusting that a boat engine would work the same way a car's did, she turned the key and felt the powerful surge of the motors. There were several gears and levers and she jerked at them randomly.

The boat lurched suddenly forward, cutting in an arc and almost capsizing. Lily hit the panel of switches with such force that it knocked the breath out of her. She could only hope that she'd given Wayman and the thugs an equal dose of bruises.

She grabbed the wheel in an attempt to straighten the boat. The vessel was so finely crafted that it responded to her slightest touch. She over-corrected and felt the boat veering toward the shore.

"Damn," she said, easing the wheel back. She knew she had only seconds before the thugs would be after her. She'd never have time to negotiate the narrow channel to the river. She could hear them crashing and cursing on the stairs. She flipped the wheel again, this time holding on to it for dear life. She heard a satisfactory thumping from the stairs. Yes! The erratic veering of the boat had toppled the two thugs.

"Meow!" Clotilde cried.

She aimed the boat out into the center of the inlet. There was no traffic here, but she knew she was in a private inlet.

"Hey!" She heard Wayman's furious cry. "Stop the boat now or I put a bullet into your detective friend!"

Lily jerked the wheel hard, heading back toward shore. If they were going to die, she's do as much damage as she possibly could.

A gunshot echoed in the night, reverberating over the water. Lily felt her heart stop. She corrected the boat and sent it spinning in a circle back in deeper water.

"Me-ow!" Clotilde knocked a coil of rope loose. She bit the knot and brought it to Lily.

Using the rope, Lily tied the wheel in a tight circle, kicked the motor into high, and slipped to the door of the wheelhouse, hanging on for dear life as the boat spun. Outside, the deck looked empty in the moonlight. She could still hear the gunshot in her mind, and she had to see if Mel had been injured.

The deck was treacherous with the boat spinning in such a tight circle. Before she was halfway across, one of the thugs came out of the stairway. He was limping, but he still held his gun. The second man came out on his heels. Lily froze.

They saw her instantly. She made a dash back toward the wheelhouse, but she felt a man's hand close on her neck. The last thing she felt was a fierce bang on the side of her head. Then her world slipped to blackness.

MEL FELT THE BOAT shift to a stop and didn't wait for another opportunity. He'd figured out what had happened—Lily had taken over the wheel and now she'd been captured. It was time for action. He lunged at Wayman.

The two of them fell back to the floor. Mel landed on top, but Wayman had managed to pull the gun into his chest. The cold steel barrel prodded into his sternum just below his heart.

Using all of his strength, Mel flipped himself over. He held Wayman in a grip so tight he hoped to crush the air out of his lungs. When Mel had pulled the other man on top of him, he used his right hand to knock the gun. The weapon discharged and Mel felt a burning pain sear his shoulder.

The gun clattered across the floor, and Mel ignored his throbbing shoulder as he scrambled to his knees and lunged after the weapon. His fingers were almost at it when he felt the pressure of a high heel in the back of his hand.

"Not so fast," Margie said. She leveled a smaller pistol at Mel. "Now both of you, get back against the wall." She bent down and picked up Wayman's gun. Holding both weapons pointed at the men, she eased toward the door.

"You made a mistake when you hit me, Wayman," she said. "I always thought Susie was the nagging bitch you made her out to be. Now I'm thinking I made an error in judgment. You just like to hit women."

Wayman rose to his feet. "Don't be stupid, Margie. I have a bad temper. It's something I can work on."

"You're a murderer, Wayman Bishop. You'd kill me just like you would your wife or anyone else who gets in your way."

"Margie, that's not true." Wayman started toward her.

Margie pulled the hammer back on her smaller gun. "It's only a .32, but I daresay I can hit a vital spot with it. If I don't kill you, I can at least slow you down a lot."

"Put the gun down!" Wayman's voice cracked like a whip. The anger he'd been trying to check came out in his tone and contorted face. "I'm not going to tell you again. Put that damn gun down and get over here.''

"I don't like the way you talk to me," Margie said, backing slowly toward the door.

Mel watched the scene, wondering how far Margie would go. Had she truly seen Wayman for the monster he was? He had to make a choice—to trust her or not.

"Get over here!" Wayman shouted.

Margie flinched, but she didn't move toward him.

Mel made up his mind. "Margie, you can do yourself a lot of good here. Give me the guns. You have my word that I'll do everything in my power to help you."

"Get. Over. Here. Right. This. Minute." Wayman spoke each word through gritted teeth.

"Or what, Wayman?" Margie asked calmly. "What will you do? Beat me again? Blacken my other eye? Tear me down a little each day until there's nothing left of me? Reduce me to the point that I'd be willing to give up my baby to protect him? I must have been insane not to see what you've done to Susie."

The door behind Margie burst open and the two men rushed inside at Margie. Wayman lunged across the room at her. Margie calmly pulled the trigger just as one of the henchmen grabbed her. The bullet hit the floor and ricocheted into Wayman's knee. He went down with a staggering groan.

As the henchmen swarmed Margie, both guns went flying out of her hands. She screamed as she was thrown against the wall. The .38 slid to the center of the room and the smaller .32 went beneath a cabinet. With the breath knocked out of her, Margie slid to the floor beside the writhing Wayman.

Mel dove for the .38, but he wasn't as fast as Wayman's thug. His fingers were almost on the grip when the gun went spinning across the floor, kicked by the henchman.

His shoulder burned as if it was on fire, but Mel rolled away from the thug and went after the gun. He knew he wasn't fast enough. He was just gaining his feet when the thug reached down and picked up the weapon. He stood up and grinned at Mel.

"Kill him," Wayman said. He clutched his knee. "Kill them all. Her, too." He pointed at Margie, who was finally getting her breath back in heaving gasps.

"How?" the hired gun asked.

"Shoot the women, then we'll burn the boat. I think we can make it appear that the detective here shot them and then tried to cover it up. But he was, unfortunately, trapped inside the boat." Wayman pushed himself to his feet. Blood oozed down his leg, but he limped over to a chair. "Just hurry up. I need medical attention."

"What about, the, uh, baby?" the thug asked.

"My son?" Wayman asked pointedly.

"Sure. And what about Susie?"

Wayman gave him a cold look. "She's outlived her usefulness. Kill her, too. In fact, do that first and bring me the kid. And get Benny to take this boat back to the dock. I don't know where that nosy reporter has gone, but find her. How did she manage to get to the wheelhouse?''

The man grinned. ''Don't worry about her. She's tied up like a Christmas turkey, and the boat is under control.'' He handed the .38 to Wayman and the two henchmen hurried out of the room.

Mel shifted to try and staunch the flow of blood from his shoulder. ''I don't think my gunshot wound will fit in very nicely with your story,'' he pointed out.

''That's my worry, isn't it?'' Wayman said. ''The good thing is you won't be alive to see if I manage it or not.''

Mel looked around the room. It seemed he was defeated, but he couldn't give up. Lily was somewhere on the boat. She'd started the engines. She was still alive, and he couldn't give up trying to save them all.

He heard the low growl and thought for a moment that he was imagining things. Then he knew exactly who it was. From beneath the cabinet Familiar's black paw snaked out and then disappeared. Familiar was under the cabinet! With the gun!

''Oh,'' Mel moaned and leaned forward. ''I think I'm going to be sick.''

''Some tough cop you are,'' Wayman ridiculed him.

''I'm sick,'' Mel groaned as he lay down on his uninjured side and extended his fingers toward the cabinet. Checking surreptitiously, he could see that his fingers were only inches away from the space where the gun had disappeared.

''Get up,'' Wayman ordered him. ''We're moving down below.''

"I'm sick," Mel moaned. "Really." He started to make retching noises and crawled toward the cabinet, twisting onto his side again.

Quick as a flash the gun shot out from under the cabinet and right into his hand. Mel rolled over, hiding the gun beneath his stomach.

"Get up." Wayman hobbled over to Mel. "I'll shoot you here. I can always come up with a new plan."

"Okay," Mel gasped. He rose to his hands and knees, his body blocking the gun from Wayman's view. Ignoring the torment of his shoulder, Mel rolled into Wayman's legs with such force that he knocked him down. Mel scrambled to his feet. This time he had the gun pointed at Wayman's head. He quickly kicked the other weapon out of reach.

"I don't really have a lot of time for this," Mel said, almost regretfully. Without any warning, he brought the butt of the gun down hard on Wayman's head. The political advisor slumped into unconsciousness.

Mel picked up both weapons and went to check Margie. She stared at him.

"Don't give me reason to regret not knocking you out," he warned her.

"I won't."

"And don't try anything stupid."

"I think I've had my quota for a lifetime," she said dismally.

Mel couldn't deny it. She was in a mess. But she

wasn't his concern. Lily was. Lily and Susie and the baby.

"How many men work for Wayman?"

"Just two are on the boat. Benny and Charles. There are others, though. Lots of them."

"Do you know how to work the radio on the boat?"

"I can try." She got to her feet slowly. "Will you really help me?" she asked.

"Help yourself," he answered. "Call the police and tell them to get here now. The past can't be undone, but we can end it here."

"Yeah." She walked out of the room without a backward glance at Wayman. He was out cold. She kicked him once for good measure.

"Meow!"

Mel looked down at the black cat who had materialized at his side. He checked Wayman one more time. He looked around the cabin but there was nothing handy to tie him up with and the smell of gasoline was strong. If Lily was below deck and the men started a fire—he had no time to lose. "Ready?" he asked Familiar.

"Meow."

"Then let's do it."

"Meow!"

IT'S SHOW TIME! I know Mel isn't one of those Miami Vice *kind of cops, but I wish he'd use a little cooler language. I mean, he's so darn traditional. But I guess right now, some solid, traditional police work is what's required.*

Lily is down there with Susie and the baby. I wonder how hard Wayman's hired henchmen will fight? I hope they give up easily. I mean, they're in this for a pay-check. Maybe they have the attitude that they aren't paid enough to get shot or killed.

I realize it's a little worry, what with everything else going on, but down in the belly of a boat isn't the place for flying bullets. I know they make these vessels to float, but it seems that if the forces of good and evil get to drilling the hull with lead, the boat might spring leaks. Yuck. Water! Nasty old river water at that.

We're below the water level, too. Which means we might get trapped. Drowning isn't exactly a cat's idea of the best route to paradise.

Here we go. It's as silent as a tomb down here. I left Clotilde up on top to keep an eye on Margie and Wayman. Surely Margie is too smart to run. Then again, she is a humanoid. It's likely she could have a panic attack and do something completely bipedal. Is that a word? Well, it should be.

I hear Benny and Charles. They're talking to Susie. They're trying to take the baby from her! She's fighting tooth and nail. Go, Susie, go!

Mel's on the move now. I think this is the time when I need to slip in front of him and stage the initial attack. I'm sort of like those sci-fi catbirds. I just launch myself and aim for the head.

Here goes! I've got Benny! He's yowling and jumping and I'm on him like white on rice! Charles is trying to figure out what's happening. Go, Mel! He's a real fighting machine. Sly Stallone could take some lessons from him. That man has more moves than Batman. He's fighting for his lady love, and let me say he is something to watch.

Yes, indeed, Mel has Charles begging for mercy. Kabam! Another one bites the dust. Time to evacuate. I'll leap to the safety of the hallway and—kabam! Mel kayos the last little bit of fight out of Benny, too. I think it was helpful that my razor-sharp claws dug enough trenches in his head so that blood got in his eyes, but it was Mel who delivered the knockout punches. Lily would be so proud of him!

Whew! That part is over, thank goodness. And Susie is wailing and crying, as is baby David. And Lily! Poor Lily, she's tied so tightly she can only wiggle. Which has instantly attracted Mel's attention.

I have to say, the man is good with knots. He's got her hands free, and now her feet. And she's standing and...rushing into his arms.

Reunion! What a wonderful sight. Lily is melting into his arms. What a kiss! Man, that heat could boil the river. And Susie is finally smiling. Even baby David has quit yowling and is cooing appropriately. Looks like a happy ending is in sight for everyone. Maybe I should go back upstairs and bite Wayman a time or two just for good measure. Maybe a nice set of fang marks on each fingertip. That would be good for him.

Or as a second alternative, what about something to eat? Clotilde and I have skipped more meals than the law allows. The kitty-cat union will be on the warpath. You know, all cats, at the moment of adoption by humanoids, sign a union contract that says we must eat every three hours. Preferably something rich and hard to obtain. So far, Clotilde and I have violated the terms. Now would be a good time for…snapper. Or shrimp. Or something exotic. Say sushi.

What's that smell?

It's vaguely acrid, sort of like…fire!

Chapter Eighteen

Lily opened her eyes as Mel suddenly ended the kiss. She'd been so happy to see him, so relieved and joyful and delighted. Blood soaked his jacket, but he insisted it was a minor injury. Was it worse than he'd said? She searched his eyes for a reason for his sudden stillness. All thoughts of safety vanished as some basic instinct warned her of danger. She could feel Mel's body reacting to the same thing.

"Get Susie and get off the boat," he said very calmly.

Suddenly Lily smelled it—smoke. She looked to see both of the cats headed to the passageway. They gave a yowl and hurried back to her.

Mel, too, crossed the small room and ducked into the hallway. He was instantly back, and she could read the worry on his face.

"The stairway is on fire," he said. "It looks like Wayman poured something flammable on it. I should have tied Wayman and Margie up," he said regretfully. "I thought she was smarter than that." He looked at Lily and shook his head. "Although I do know this has nothing to do with intelligence."

Lily felt a surge of pride. Mel was a man capable of understanding. Once he got hold of something, he really made it his own.

"We need to find a fire extinguisher." Lily put thought into action and began opening the cabinets in the bathroom.

"Is there another way up on deck?" Mel asked Susie.

"I don't know. I stayed on the boat with Wayman a few times, but he was so controlling. I never explored."

"Meow!" Clotilde put a paw on one of the henchmen. "Meow!"

Familiar joined her, batting the man in the face with his paw, claws sheathed.

"Good idea!" Lily said. She went into the bathroom and came out with a glass of water. Without a second's hesitation, she threw it on the thug named Charles. He came to consciousness sputtering and swearing. It was only when he heard the click of the hammer on Mel's gun that he shut up and looked around him. Then he sniffed.

"You boss has set the boat on fire in the hopes that all of us, including you and Benny, will burn to death. You want to give us some help? Maybe tell us where there's a fire extinguisher or another route of escape?" Mel asked.

Charles seemed to think about it for a moment. "There's a commercial extinguisher in the wheelhouse."

"What about another route to the deck?" Mel asked.

He shook his head. "Only exit is the stairs." He sniffed again. "How bad is the fire?"

"We can't get through it," Lily said. Her heart was pounding. There had to be a way. After everything they'd been through, they couldn't simply sit down and burn to death. She glanced over at Susie who was rocking little David in her arms.

"If I'd left him with the Johnsons, he would have had a chance to live," she said. "You were right all along, Lily."

"We'll get out of this," Mel vowed. "We will."

Lily went to Mel and laced her arm through his. "We made a promise to each other, and we can't go back on it now."

She was rewarded with a look from Mel that spoke volumes of his love for her. "We will make it," he said, leaning down to kiss her cheek.

There was a noise above them, a sound like hissing. Lily looked at Mel and saw his worry. Was Wayman up there turning on butane tanks?

"Hey!" The voice came to them dimly from above. "Hey! Are you alive?"

"It's Margie," Lily and Mel said in unison.

"Ye-ow!" Familiar scampered into the passageway. "Yeow!"

Lily and Mel were right on his heels. Flames were eating away at the stairs and walls and framed in the orange glow was Margie Levert. She held up the fire extinguisher. "I can't operate it," she said. "You can." She heaved it down the stairwell to Mel, who caught it with a groan as the strain tore at his shoulder.

In a few seconds he was directing the spray of foam at the stairs, fighting the blazing flames. "Stay back," he warned Lily. "Wayman had gasoline. That's what I smelled."

Lily stood behind him, unable to do a thing as Mel battled the intense heat of the fire. Just as she was about to give up hope, Mel brought the flames under control. He tossed the extinguisher aside and started up the stairway, testing to make sure it would hold the weight of the others. "Where's Wayman?" he called up to Margie.

"He jumped ship. He came to while I was radioing for help. When I came out to check on him, he had already started the fire, and then he leaped over the rail. I guess he swam to shore. In the darkness I couldn't see where he went," Margie said. She held out a hand to Mel and pulled him on deck.

Mel helped Lily out and called down to the others to hurry.

In the distance, they heard the whir of a helicopter.

"I think they're sending a swat team," Margie said. "When I saw the fire I radioed back and told them what was happening."

Mel put a hand on her shoulder. "Thank you, Margie. I will do what I can for you. That's a promise."

"Find Wayman Bishop and put him behind bars. I may serve time, too, but I'll do it with a glad heart if I know he's also in jail. He lied to me. I can't believe I was so foolish. I believed everything he said." She wiped a tear from her face. "It was all Susie. She was lying and cheating on him and trying to steal his money. The things he made me believe." She went to Susie, who held her baby tightly in her arms. "I'm so sorry."

"I believed him, too," Susie said. "At first I wanted to believe what he said about other people. Then when he started on me, I believed all of those ugly things, too. Until finally I didn't want to believe, but I didn't have enough confidence not to. If anyone can understand how it happens, I can."

Lily went to Susie. "Whatever else, you've gotten something back that no one will ever take away from you again. Yourself."

"And my baby," Susie said. "I think it might have killed me to lose David."

"That's not going to be a problem now," Mel assured her. "But let's get back to the dock and find Wayman."

The helicopter burst over the treetops and a flood-light struck the deck of the boat. Mel waved a signal that they were safe and went to the radio to let them know that a manhunt for Wayman Bishop was the next order of business.

The boat had drifted to the far side of the river, and Mel started the engines. He slowly turned the boat and headed back for the dock.

"I can manage from here," Margie said, taking the wheel from him.

Lily saw that he was reluctant to give up the wheel. She went to his side and gently touched him. Blood soaked his shirt. He was hurt a lot worse than he'd let on. "It's over, Mel. You've got the bad guys. Let's go to the cabin," she said softly.

Before he could protest, she led him away from the others. Only Familiar and Clotilde followed. When she closed the door, she finally turned to him.

"How bad is it?" she asked. She unbuttoned his shirt and pulled the fabric back to reveal a severe wound. Blood still oozed from it.

Lily bit back the cry of fear. She quickly found towels and began to apply pressure to the wound to staunch the bleeding.

She felt the boat gently bump the dock and realized that Margie was as good as her word. Good. As soon as they were on solid land, she wanted paramedics and an ambulance. Mel had lost a lot of blood. Even now, though he was about to fall over, he insisted on remaining upright. Well, he was one hardheaded man. She'd known it since she first met him. It was a trait they shared, and one that she knew she would see again in the future—because she intended to have a future with Mel.

The wa-wa of sirens cut the night and she smiled at Mel. "The cavalry is here," she said, brushing his dark hair back from his forehead and kissing him.

"Not a moment too soon," he admitted.

"What about Wayman?" she asked.

"He doesn't stand a chance. He can run, but they'll find him. And with Margie willing to turn state's evidence against him, he'll spend the rest of his days in jail."

"And Susie?"

"I think she and the baby can count on the fact that their future together will never be jeopardized again."

Lily bent down and kissed Mel tenderly. "What about our future?"

"Now that we both admit we want one together, I don't think there's anything that can stand in our way."

LILY LOOKED UP as the door of the hospital room swung open yet again. Already the room was filled to overcrowding. Mel's boss had just left, along with half a dozen detectives.

She still held the newspaper that her boss had dropped by with a front-page headline that read, Abuse of Power at All Levels: Wayman Bishop Arrested. Lily's byline was prominently displayed.

Lowering the newspaper, Lily was a little surprised to see Preston and Rose Johnson enter the room with a huge bouquet of tulips.

"We hope you're feeling better," Rose said.

"I'm fine," Mel said, his voice gruff with embarrassment. "It was only a flesh wound. I don't know why they made me stay here."

Lily rolled her eyes. "He almost died, and he was lucky to keep his arm. But, of course, that's only a flesh wound."

Mel reached out and caught her hand, drawing her to the hospital bed. "When I'm well, I'm going to teach you proper respect for the man who loves you."

"I can't wait," Lily said, her delight impossible to hide. She kissed him lightly, wanting so much more. But there wasn't a moment alone.

The door opened again.

"Babs!" She'd forgotten her sister was due to arrive for the weekend—and with a tall, slender man wearing glasses. The writer!

"Lily, this is Luke. Luke, my sister, the woman who helps put abusive men behind bars where they belong." She leaned over to whisper in Lily's ear, "A little bird named Mel called me and told me to meet you here."

Lily made the introductions all around. She eyed her sister's boyfriend and found that against all of her earlier prejudices, she liked what she saw. Babs had changed. Luke was as different from Bobby Reynolds as day was from night. Babs deserved love. Luckily, she was also brave enough to try again.

There was a tap on the door and Eleanor Curry peeped in. "A full house," she said, pushing open the door and entering. Peter followed her. They both carried plastic carriers.

"Familiar and Clotilde insisted," Eleanor said. "I'm sure they could have gotten in here by themselves, but medical environments make Familiar a little nervous. He decided to let me and Peter help." As she talked she unlatched the carrier door and Familiar leaped onto the bed with Mel. Peter released Clotilde, who also jumped onto the bed.

"Welcome," Mel said, scratching first one and then the other.

Lily picked up Familiar and kissed the top of his head. "What a cat," she said. "I'd take either or both of them in a heartbeat."

"No way," Eleanor said. "There are times Familiar

worries me sick, but I wouldn't trade a hair on his magnificent head.''

There was one more timid knock and the door swung open to reveal Susie and little David.

For a moment Lily felt a pang of sympathy for Rose and Preston Johnson. How unfortunate that they should be here when Susie visited with the baby. She felt true remorse at hurting such good people.

"Susie!" Rose and Preston cried, getting up to hug the young woman. In an instant Rose had the baby in her arms, cooing and tickling the infant into peals of laughter.

Lily looked at Mel, who beamed back at her.

"Okay, I think we're all here and ready," Mel said. "Not too long ago I thought I would be announcing that Lily was in serious trouble for aiding in the abandonment of a baby. After all, we all know who left little David at the Johnsons' home, don't we?" He gave her a long look. "But in the course of this case, I learned a few things about Lily, and a lot about myself. Now I find that I'm prepared to rethink the future.''

Lily looked around at the smiling faces. Obviously everyone there knew what was going on—except her. "Mel?" she asked, looking from face to face. No one volunteered a word.

Mel pressed the buzzer and the already jammed room was even more packed as nurses and orderlies wheeled in a cart. Instead of medical supplies, it was loaded with bottles of chilled champagne and glasses.

"Doctor's orders," Mel said, raising his eyebrows

as he handed a glass to Lily. When everyone had a drink he sat up taller in the bed.

"This isn't the position I thought I'd be in when I did this, but I wanted all of you here to…help me persuade Lily of the rightness of this idea."

She saw the mischief in his dancing eyes, and she did her best to control the smile that teased the corners of her mouth. "I don't think the doctor would approve of all this excitement," she said staunchly.

"To the contrary," Mel said, "he has recommended this course of action."

"What action?" Lily was dying to know, but she knew she had to wait until Mel was ready to tell her.

"Lily," Mel took her hand and raised it to his lips, "will you marry me?"

It was the question she'd dreamed he'd ask, but Lily suddenly was unprepared to answer. She tried to speak, but there wasn't any air left in her lungs. She looked at Mel in the hospital bed, still pale from his close brush with death, and her heart hurt so painfully that tears came to her eyes.

"Lily, it isn't a death sentence," Mel said. He tried for a light note but there was disappointment in his voice. He looked around the room at the expectant faces. "Maybe this wasn't such a good idea."

"Wait!" Lily squeezed his hand, holding on for dear life. "The only death sentence would be living without you, Mel. It's just that…" she took a breath, "I'm so happy I don't know what to say."

"Try yes!" Mel stage-whispered.

"Yes!" she said. "Yes!" she shouted. "Yes, yes, yes!"

"I think it's an official engagement," Babs said. "And out of graciousness as the older sister, I might have to let her beat me to the altar. Let's drink up." She held up her champagne glass. "To happy futures, and to men and women who know the true meaning of love."

After everyone had drunk the toast, Preston Johnson cleared his throat loudly. "Rose and I have an announcement, too." They linked hands, the baby still in Rose's arms. Preston pulled Susie and the baby forward to stand with them.

"Susie has agreed to live with us while she plans a new future. We're going to be David's unofficial godparents."

Susie stepped forward and lifted her champagne glass. "The world is full of wonderful, loving people. Thanks to Lily and Mel, I let them into my life. To Lily and Mel."

"Me-ow!" Familiar said indignantly.

"And to Familiar and Clotilde," Susie hastily amended.

AH, THERE'S NOTHING MORE joyful in life than a roomful of humanoids who know the value of a cat. I'm positive Eleanor and Peter can find a little stray kitten at the pound for the newly engaged couple. A purr-fect wedding present, if you get my drift.

I'm delighted Susie and little David are going to remain in the neighborhood. Intuition tells me that Rose and Preston will have plenty of lap time with that infant. And Susie will have a safe harbor. It couldn't have worked out better if I'd planned it my-self.

They're passing the bubbly around again. Now I appreciate the little crystal dish of champagne they poured for me and Clotilde, but I'm actually more interested in a heartier fare. And nothing from the hospital kitchen, please!

Mel and Lily can live on love, but Clotilde and I want something from the sea.

Wait a minute, though, she's giving me that green vixen look. I do think all of the bubbly she drank has gone to her head. What a little minx. She's winking at me.

I think it's time for us to find our way home. The house is empty and we'll have the run of the place. First a little romance and then some chow.

Okay, my gorgeous feline, let's let the humanoids celebrate while we find our own entertainment. And I suppose I have to also give my baby kitty a few licks and purrs for her excellent detective work. I had my doubts that such a feminine creature could hold up to the strenuous work of detecting, but Clotilde came through with flying colors.

What a gal! What a cat! What an adventure!

Harlequin Romance®
Love affairs that last a lifetime.

HARLEQUIN® Presents®
Seduction and passion guaranteed.

Harlequin® Historical
Historical Romantic Adventure.

HARLEQUIN® Temptation.
Sassy, sexy, seductive!

HARLEQUIN® Super Romance®
Emotional, exciting, unexpected.

HARLEQUIN® AMERICAN Romance®
Heart, home & happiness.

HARLEQUIN® Duets™
Romantic comedy.

HARLEQUIN® INTRIGUE®
Breathtaking romantic suspense.

Get caught reading Harlequin.

HARLEQUIN®
Makes any time special®

In August 2001

New York Times bestselling author

TESS GERRITSEN

joins

ANNETTE BROADRICK

&

Mary Lynn Baxter

in

TAKE5

Volume 4

These five riveting love stories are quick reads, great escapes and guarantee five times the suspense.

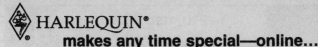

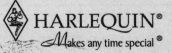